Addicted To Love:

An Eastside Love Story

by

Nina Michelle

COPYRIGHT PAGE

Dedication

This book is dedicated to all of the women out there who have been crazy in love and somehow lost themselves along the way. Sometimes it takes life's ups and downs for you to figure out how to totally love yourself and love someone else too! Here's to surviving being Addicted To Love!!!

The Beginning

Cadence and Bo! This was it! Cadence had met the man who would make her dreams of Happily Ever After come true.

"Who would have known working out at your nearest YMCA could give you the opportunity of a lifetime." Cadence thought.

Well, it was the place she met Bo. Bo was a self-proclaimed player who thought he had an ear to the streets. He was a tall man about 5'7, and brown skin like the color of the crunch on the inside of a Twix. He kept his hair in braids and dressed as if he was auditioning for a 90's music video every time you laid eyes on him.

Cadence was delusional, but she fell for Bo, because he gave her the attention she longed for. Being a product of a single mother really played on Cadence's emotions. She NEEDED something, and Bo was right there to fill the void. He took Cadence out on dates, showed her off in public, and even invited her to meet his mother. Cadence thought this was the real deal. After 5 months of dating she committed herself to Bo, and began to express love the best way she knew how.

One night Bo took Cadence out to the movies. After the most gentlemanly display of car door opening, hand holding, and just plain courting Cadence just knew this was the real deal. Bo asked Cadence to return to his house to spend the night.

Cadence hesitated although she was a grown woman she never really opened herself up to spend the night with men or have sex.

She was still a hopeless romantic waiting on Mr. Right to come and sweep her off of her feet.

"I know this is it for me being with Bo, but it's my FIRST time!" Cadence chuckled to herself.

Cadence then looked at Bo. He smiled ever so softly and she melted.

"I would love to spend the night with you Bo."

Bo continued to be a gentleman and he took her to his place. It was on this night that Cadence lost a piece of her innocence that would never return. Cadence's first experience wasn't terribly bad, but she still felt alone.

She thought to herself how could she be alone in a room with a man whom she just gave herself to?

She forced herself to turn over and face the wall and fall asleep, even though all she wanted to do was crawl home and cry about the mistake she had just made.

As the morning sun shone through the window Cadence heard the doorbell to Bo's house ringing hysterically. As Cadence got up to go to the washroom she heard a female voice.

"I know you have a trick in there Bo!" screamed a woman from the door.

"Tiny baby why would there be anyone in here with me when you are the only woman who has my heart!" Bo exclaimed

Cadence laughed loudly. "You have got to be kidding me!" She yelled from the bathroom.

"Bo if you don't let me in this house I'm going to cut you right here and right now!" Tiny was livid. She knew Bo was a cheater, but she had never caught him. This was all the fuel she needed for her fire.

"I can't let you do that Tiny!" Bo tried to keep a straight face.

Cadence grabbed her things from Bo's room and summoned an Uber from her phone. 2 minutes until arrival her phone read. Cadence walked toward the door and pushed past Bo as forcefully as she could almost making him fall into Tiny.

"You are a complete and utter jackass!" "And to think I thought you were my Happily Ever After when you're more like Nightmare on Elm Street!" Cadence scoffed at Bo.

"Happily Ever After! How long have you been with this nigga?" Tiny asked, perplexed.

"5 months! But I'm done you can have him!" Cadence replied with a sense of anger and hurt! She had just lost her virginity to this douchebag only to be confronted by his girl less than 24 hours later.

"I don't want him either." Tiny screamed as she walked off to her car.

Cadence was now too pissed she had to wait on an Uber that was taking forever to arrive. She could feel Bo staring at her wanting to say something, but couldn't find the words to say.

Cadence could no longer take the prolonged stares and decided to walk to the corner store to wait for the Uber instead. She retrieved her phone from her bag and continued to walk head down texting the Uber driver to notify him that she was going to be picked up from the corner store instead. As soon as she pressed send she looked up it was too late. Cadence had run smack dead into the back of a man who was walking backwards talking, she fell back from the force.

"Damn baby, I'm sorry!" "I'm so busy trying to run my mouth I ain't paid a lick of attention to what's going on! "Khalil said with a sly look on his face.

Cadence looked up at Khalil. He was tall. Dark. And Fine. A lethal combination!

He reached down to help Cadence up. He pulled her to her feet with one hand and helped her stabilize herself.

"You gotta be more careful baby girl! To be aware is to be alive."

Cadence couldn't even concentrate on the amazing specimen of a man that was before her!

"Whatever!" Was all she could muster given the circumstances.

"Damn that's how you feel baby girl?" Khalil said intently.

"Well good day to you too!" Khalil looked Cadence up and down and gave her smirk and returned to his activities. He had no time for nonsense.

By this time Cadence was infuriated. Pissed because the Uber hadn't arrived yet. Pissed because Bo was a jackass, and she found out hours too late, and pissed because how was she supposed to unlove him?

The Uber driver pulled up slowly looking around anxiously for his driver. The neighborhood was terrible and Cadence was sure he wanted an escape.

Cadence waived her hand in an attempt to get his attention as he had just slightly drove past her. She walked up a bit to catch up with the eager Uber driver, and went to grab the door.

"HEY, shorty! If I was your man I would at least take you home!" Khalil jokingly said as he watched her from the corner.

Cadence turned toward the voice and looked so intently that she was sure he could feel it in his soul. She flipped him the bird, got in the back seat of the Uber and slammed the door.

Khalil took a seat on the mailbox thinking about the rude chick that just flipped him the bird and hopped in the car. Khalil was the man! He was being groomed by Kenneth and Kane the hood superstars so life was ridiculously crazy for him at this point. He had become the hood protégé. As he sat there on the mailbox he drifted into deep thought!

"I have to assemble a team!" "Who could I trust to help me run the hood correctly?" Khalil thought for a moment!

"CHEESE and RALPH!" He was so caught in his thoughts that he didn't realize that he had said it out loud. "This will be my team."

Khalil understood that to be successful in this hood game he needed to create a team. He selected these two for very different reasons. Ralph was loyal. Ralph would never turn on Khalil; he was like the brother he never had. Cheese was a different story. Cheese was Khalil's attachment and he felt an undying obligation to him.

The slight breeze Khalil felt sitting on the mailbox drifted him back to thinking about his childhood. He closed his eyes for a moment and lifted his head.

He thought about how Cheese had been around since he was ten and he felt like he was his brother. He knew from the beginning Cheese was cut from a different cloth, but he felt a need to protect him. He groomed him for the streets, but Cheese wasn't all together ready. Khalil saw some potential and went forth with the idea against his gut feeling.

The team was assembled and it was time to do what Khalil knew best; get money.

Khalil opened his eyes and hopped off the mailbox. He walked around the corner to the "trap house" to see Kenneth and Kane to get his product. They gave it to him for a cheaper price since he was next in line to hold down the block. Khalil, Cheese, and Ralph all worked together to get rid of the product as swiftly as possible. They were like the damn dream team when it came to the neighborhood drug game. They got the product and got rid of it within the week, and then Khalil went back to see Kenneth and Kane.

Kenneth and Kane were superbly impressed by how efficient Khalil's team was. Khalil would require every hundred dollars to be put away to go back to the store and at the end of the night they emptied their pockets of singles. All singles were placed in a garbage bag and used at the weeks end for their lofty excursions.

Those excursions included nights on the town, clubs, liquor, weed, and of course women. Women were no problem for Khalil and the crew. They had flocks of them. All shapes, sizes, and nationalities. These women were ready and willing to do any and everything to be a part of the team or at least have the delusion of being a part of something. Khalil was not quick to let people in, and women were disposable to him. He got them, used them for his pleasure, and put them on the shelf for a rainy day if ever he needed them again.

Khalil was very strategic about not hurting people's feelings, because he was so kind hearted. He also made sure to never choose a side. Khalil had a way of keeping women around, befriending them, and making them feel at ease. He had a way of making you feel like you were in a relationship even though he committed to no one. He would treat you like a Queen while you were in his presence one minute, and dismiss you in the next.

Khalil trusted none.

This trait of unpredictability was passed down from Kaleb his father, and Khalil honed it to perfection. Khalil could truly love a woman and show no emotion behind it. He always expected the worst so he was prepared in case it happened.

The dream team was at an all-time high; they were living the life they always imagined and in their eyes nothing could bring them down. What they didn't know was that life was about to throw a blow that would knock the wind out of them.

Chapter 1

Cadence reached her front door. "Why the hell was she seeing Bo again?" She thought to herself.

He quietly whispered "I love you Cadence." As if he had just read the question she asked herself in her mind.

Cadence looked at Bo with a blank stare. Her stare was so unconcerned because she could not figure out how she had gotten here. Why was she still sleeping with this man KNOWING he was having sex with someone else! She had looked through Bo's phone last night while he was in the washroom. She knew what he had been up to. Bo had been texting Tiny for weeks. The messages between Tiny and Bo were pretty extensive too. Cadence even saw a message where Bo told Tiny he loved her too.

Cadence thought "How could I be so dumb?"

She thought about how much of a scrub Bo was and began to get so infuriated she started crying!

Bo tried to console her, but she just wanted to be left alone. Cadence pulled away and looked out the window for a minute.

She began to open the door, and said "Whatever Bo I love you too." Lying to herself and him simultaneously.

Bo blew Cadence a kiss and said "call me when you can okay."

Cadence nodded her head and proceeded to put the key in the door. She entered her apartment and began to cry.

"What the fuck is wrong with you?" She yelled to herself.

She thought about how she gave herself to Bo and he was such a lying bum. She thought about why Bo was entertaining Tiny, and why he would cheat on her. Cadence's head began to pound with all the questions she was asking herself. She couldn't believe the situation she was in, and she couldn't even call anyone to let them know how much of a dumb ass move she had made for fear of embarrassment. She knew she was being stupid, but she didn't know how to undue the stupidity. How would she get out of this hole that she dug herself into?

Khalil and the dream team were living the life. They were making money, saving money, and spending money like it was their new past time.

Kenneth and Kane went out of town to reload on the product.

Khalil, Cheese, and Ralph waited patiently. Khalil decided to have a meeting so he could ensure that everyone was on the same page. Cheese and Ralph came over to his crib.

Ralph closed the door behind them and they each took a seat.

Khalil stood by the door.

Ralph sat on a chair looking at Khalil, and Cheese sat on the bed.

Cheese smiled and said "What's up bro." "Why are you looking so serious?"

Khalil replied "This is serious!" "It's money making time."

Cheese and Ralph looked perplexed.

Ralph replied "We've been making money Khalil."

Khalil nodded in agreement and said "Yeah Yeah I know, but I'm talking real money! "When Kenneth and Kane come back from

OT we're going to be on a whole nother level." I talked to Kane before he left and he said we've been performing so well he's going to front us the weed, and put us in the game with the Diesel."

Cheese's eyes lit up like a kid on Christmas. "I know they ain't finna snap like that?" Asked Cheese.

Khalil replied "Yeah."

Ralph jumped up out the chair and shouted "It's on my dude."

Khalil waved his hands to get Ralph to quiet down. They had to be cautious anybody could be listening.

Khalil, Cheese and Ralph were beyond excited. They knew more money equaled: The freedom to do whatever they liked!

Khalil looked around his apartment and said "We're all done here! Let's hit the block and kick it."

Cheese and Ralph proceeded to join him.

They slowly closed the door to the studio apartment behind them and made their way to the block. They expected it to be cracking! It was hot and everybody was out, but when they walked to the corner they saw plenty of people, but everybody was crying!

Khalil shouted "What's up! What's wrong with everybody?"

Nobody could utter a word. Khalil's older sister walked up, choking back the tears. She began to talk, but kept choking. Khalil was getting pissed.

She started again "Khalil it's Kenneth and Kane."

"What?" Khalil began to hiss.

His sister continued "The plane Kenneth and Kane took out of town crashed! There were no survivors."

Khalil couldn't believe what he was hearing. He kept repeating "What?" "What?" "What?" Khalil proceeded to scream while pacing the block in total disbelief. Khalil felt like his life was over. His mentors and brothers were gone. It never even crossed Khalil's mind that everything he and the dream team had made was on that plane. They sent all of the money in its entirety to re-up. They had absolutely nothing!

Khalil decided that the best thing to do was to drink his pain away. For three days straight Khalil didn't touch a piece of food, but drank Hennessey non-stop. Hennessey brought the worst out of Khalil; he turned into the Incredible Hulk and there was no calming him down. Into his second day of binge drinking Khalil realized that he had absolutely no money to his name.

He decided to call Cheese and Ralph to discuss the plans for moving forward. When Cheese and Ralph arrived they looked at Khalil in total silence. Khalil looked as if he were a part of The Walking Dead. His eye socks were sunken as if they were the Titanic, his eyeballs were bulging like the Pine-sol lady, and the skin on his face was sagging and hanging like a pot of chitterlings.

Khalil was absent of emotion, and literally a dead man walking.

Ralph and Cheese listened intentionally as Khalil began to speak.

As Khalil opened his mouth the lingering smell of liquor exploded first. Ralph and Cheese took a deep breath, and Khalil began.

"We ain't got no money man, it's all bad y'all". I ain't been answering ya'll calls because I've been trying to think of a plan.

Khalil continued "I tried to hit a lick."

Ralph and Cheese looked crazy.

Ralph jumped up "You tried to hit a lick without us."

Khalil shook his head in agreement. "Man Ralph, I was riding getting drunk just trying to process everything that's been going on. I realized we ain't have a dime. We had sent everything on the plane with Kenneth and Kane. I was getting off the expressway on 71st and state and saw Cutty walking in the gas station.

Cheese interjected "Cutty." Khalil replied angrily "Yeah Cutty. You remember he took those poles from his brother's house that we had over there. I hadn't seen him since! He was looking like money so I upped on him." "What I didn't know was that he was there with Rito." Khalil's anger began to suppress a bit.

Rito and Khalil had been friends since the beginning of time. Their mothers attended the same church and he loved Rito. Rito was like a distant brother. He had mad respect for him, and would show nothing but love his way.

Ralph looked perplexed. "So what happened?"

Khalil continued "Well I upped the strap and told Cutty to give me the bread. Rito jumped out of the car screaming my name, and I turned to look at him, because I knew his voice." "Cutty took off running up 71st like Jesse Owens in the Olympic Gold Medal 100 yard dash." "I just watched and talked to Rito for a minute and jumped in the whip and came back over East." Ralph and Cheese both nodded.

Then Ralph spoke "So what's the plan?" Khalil sat on the end of the bed and sighed "that's what I called you here for." "For the first time ever "I don't have a plan."

Chapter 2

Cadence knew that getting over Bo was going to be tough. She needed a move of God to help her with that task. She decided to go burn some steam at the YMCA working out or even running a quick game of basketball since it was one of her hobbies. She had been playing ball since she was 8 years old, and it served as her escape from reality!

As Cadence entered the door she was greeted by a couple of her friends. Cadence smiled from ear to ear, and looked around frantically.

She turned to K and said "So what's been up?"

K looked at her blankly and said "nothing same ol same ol."

Cadence kept looking around and K asked "what are you looking for Cadence?"

Cadence looked at K with a school girl crush and smiled!

K dropped her head a little and said "Oh, Cadence there is something I have to tell you." Cadence looked at K intently listening because K sounded so serious.

K continued "Cadence it's Bo."

But as soon as K was about to spill the beans in walked Bo with his crew Junior and Carl. Cadence couldn't understand why she still was slightly happy to see Bo. After all the mess she still felt something for him. Maybe it was because she gave him her virginity or maybe because she had Daddy issues. Whatever it was Cadence couldn't quite shake him.

She remembered that K was telling her something, and turned and said "K we'll finish later okay."

K looked puzzled and said "Cadence", but decided to let her go anyway.

Cadence got up to greet Boo and give him a hug he pushed back a little and was quite distant looking at her as if he didn't know her.

Junior and Carl began to chuckle and laugh and started to walk ahead of them.

Cadence looked perplexed and asked Bo "what's up?"

Bo looked at Cadence and said "We need to talk."

Cadence knew that something was wrong, but what could it be?

Cadence thought to herself "What could I have done?" Was our last night together not good? What does he have to say?

Cadence slapped her face slightly to snap out of her thoughts "Bitch! Get it together! This nigga is playing all type of games with you, and you're asking yourself what did you do wrong!"

When they reached a corner of the gym Bo asked Cadence to take a seat on a fairly empty bench to talk. The only person there was Mikey.

Mikey was a dude who grew up with Cadence so she wasn't bothered by his presence. She just wanted to get to the bottom of things with Bo.

Cadence spoke "What's up Mikey?"

Mikey replied "Nothing Cadence you good?" looking directly at Bo. He wasn't a big fan of him or his crew!

Cadence said "Yeah I'm good Mikey!"

Mikey turned his back to them and continued to watch the old heads play ball.

Bo looked at Cadence and started "Cadence you know I love you right?"

Cadence replied "Yeah Bo I love you too." Still trying to convince herself and him!

Bo continued "I love you but, I'm not in love with you I want to be with somebody else!"

Cadence's heart fell to her feet.

Mikey's ears were perked up from eavesdropping like the FBI he wanted to turn around and say something, but he kept his back to them.

Cadence felt a lump forming in her throat. She began to speak with tears rolling down her eyes .

"Why Bo?" "Who is it?" Cadence asked rhetorical questions, because she already knew the answer. She remembered the girl at the door and the text conversations between Bo and Tiny, and she knew she had to be the reason why.

"Why the fuck do I care anyway!" Cadence thought to herself but couldn't stop the tears or questions she had from flowing freely.

Bo looked at Cadence emotionlessly.

He stated that he found a girl. He said her name was Tiny and that he loved her.

"She is beautiful and the woman for me."

Cadence began to sob.

During her moping around the house she investigated who Tiny was. She found out that she was a short brown skin girl with pretty hair. She had also found out that Tiny very young which added insult to injury!

Bo continued "We can still be friends Cadence! This doesn't mean I don't love you!" Cadence was hurt beyond belief and couldn't believe the words she was hearing from Bo's mouth! She just sat there looking stupid! What was even more delusional was that through everything that Bo had said out of his mouth Cadence only heard "But I still love you."

That was what she longed for to be loved even if the love wasn't real. Cadence mustered up the strength to tell Bo to get away from her and turned her back to him.

Bo didn't even attempt to console her! He looked for a moment and got up and left with no remorse.

Mikey kept his back to Cadence as she sobbed by herself. He didn't say a thing but the wheels in his head were turning. He said to himself "I'll fix this for you Cadence."

Khalil was stuck without having a plan at getting money. He decided to spend more time hooping since he had absolutely no reason to be on the block so tough without any work.

Spending more time at the courts he began to reunite with his old homeboy Mikey who went to the same rough neighborhood school as did. He and Mikey decided to start a crew at the courts. Khalil had the dream team on the block, but he knew since he would be on the courts more he might as well build a team there, because he knew building a team was a recipe for success.

Whatever Khalil did he put forth %150 and his plan was to run the courts. It could be a temporary way to hustle to get money since he was truly a talented basketball player. He started the crew with Mikey, Big Boy, and Jabar.

Mikey had played basketball with Khalil his entire life! They were ride or die for each other and anybody that knew them knew that if you saw one you saw the other.

Big Boy was super cool and loyal. Not much of a hooper, but would give his all to any situation. Big Boy was a medium tall chubby boy with swag. He could always be caught smiling, and even though he was big he had a spectacular way of charming the ladies. Big Boy was a jokester who really had an underlying issue with self-esteem, but hid it so well you wouldn't know unless you were observant.

Big Boy was Khalil's homey.

Jabar was a hooper! He was awkwardly tall, extremely skinny, lanky, and uncoordinated, but had great potential! Khalil knew Jabar from playing small fry, but they never really kicked it with him outside of the confines of Small Fry Ball.

This would be the team for the courts! All hustle: No play!

Khalil began to put his plan in motion.

They came to courts together and left together.

If anyone had a problem with one they had to see all four, and people started to realize they didn't want that type of trouble.

Khalil went to the courts to make money and take his mind off the tragedy from the block.

Mikey went to the courts, because there wasn't anything else to do. He had to keep his availability open because he was the sole caregiver for his sick Grandfather who raised him. Therefore, being at the courts gave him an outlet from taking care of his grandfather day in and day out.

Khalil was at the courts daily from sun up to sun down since Kenneth and Kane had died. The more Khalil, Mikey, Big Boy, and Jabar kicked it at the courts the more people flocked to them. The size of their crew started to increase rapidly and it went from four to twelve in a matter of months. Men at the courts now knew their motto well "If one fights we all fight."

At any given moment a fight could erupt in the midst of a V that would look like mob action, because of the numbers of their new found crew.

They decided to put a name to their creation and call themselves The Dirty Dozen. The name represented a lot for the guys! Although it was a membership of more than 12 the original founders were twelve members, and they decided on Dirty not because they were literally dirty, but because things could get dirty if you lead them to it. And so a gang was formed.

The gang from the courts took off just like Khalil's dream team on the block. The Dirty Dozen began to expand to other city courts. Not just Hayes! North, South, West there were no limits.

With the expansion of the "gang" came added trouble for Khalil. Trouble that he wasn't looking for, Khalil prided himself on staying in the background of things, never wanting too much attention, but attention always seemed to find him! The very thing that he was trying to hide from seemed to chase him down like a hawk, and would cause more trouble than a little bit in the months to come.

Chapter 3

Cadence could not believe that after all of this her and Bo were over. She kept replaying the conversation over and over in her head only hanging on to Bo saying, "But it doesn't mean I don't love you Cadence."

Cadence had convinced herself that Bo loved her and no matter what she was determined to make them work at any cost.

Cadence found herself calling Bo more than usual, because she missed the attention that he used to give her. She would call Bo and receive no answer, and began to cry. She cried telling herself "But Bo does love me he's just confused right now."

This notion kept Cadence full of hope, because she wanted to believe in love although she knew deep down inside this couldn't be love.

Finally, after a couple of days of calling Bo returned Cadence's call.

"What's up Cadence?" Bo said in an irritated tone.

"I've been calling you Bo." "Why haven't you answered?"

Bo's response was short and dry. "I've been busy."

Cadence began to get irritated "Busy doing what?"

Bo decided it was time to be clear about some things and held nothing back in that regard.

"Cadence we are not together anymore." He began. "You know I'm with Tiny now so why are you sweating me?"

Cadence felt like she was about to explode "Sweating you, sweating you, because I called you!" You said we were still friends, and that you still loved me or was that a lie?

Bo sighed. He knew things had ended so abruptly between him and Cadence and a part of him knew Cadence was a good woman, and he didn't want to treat her badly because she didn't deserve it, but he wanted to do him!

"Cadence, can I come and pick you up so we can talk in person?"

Cadence thought for a moment. She knew she had no business going with Bo. She knew he didn't want to talk! What did they really have to talk about? He had said everything that he needed to say. He was with Tiny! That should have been the end, but Cadence longed for someone to fill the void that she had. She wanted to be loved and she was willing to achieve that at any cost.

Cadence obliged.

Bo replied "I'm on my way."

Cadence climbed in the front seat with Bo, and her mind began to race with questions, thoughts, and anxiety. She wondered if he had just dropped off Tiny, or if he loved her more, or if he planned on breaking up with her to get Cadence back? All of the thoughts exploded into tears.

Bo looked at Cadence and began to drive.

"Why are you crying Cadence?"

The legendary throat lump returned and Cadence choked on her words! She felt so many emotions, but couldn't find a way to express any. She just couldn't believe this was happening to her.

After a ride that was absent of words, but had a presence of sobs they arrived at Bo's house. Cadence looked at Bo as if to ask why are we here.

Bo as if he read Cadence's mind replied "I just wanted us to be alone."

Bo opened the car door for Cadence as he always did, and she felt like things were back to normal.

When they entered the door Bo's mother greeted her excitedly.

"Hey baby girl!" Bo's mother gave her a big hug, and when Cadence looked to the side she saw her picture on the mantelpiece along with numerous people in Bo's family.

Cadence was so excited! She felt like this proved that she was still the one. Bo motioned his hand for Cadence to come into the room, and they began to talk.

Bo started "Cadence we are young. It's stuff I just gotta get out of my system before I settle down forever. It's not that I don't love you, because I do, but I just gotta do me."

Cadence didn't understand what "Do me!" meant. She was baffled. She wanted a further explanation, but Bo leaned in for a kiss.

Cadence hesitated, she knew deep inside that Bo was doing this with Tiny, but this was how she felt like she should express her love. So they kissed, and the kissing escalated to touching, and the touching turned into sex, and afterwards Cadence felt dumb.

Cadence and Bo did the back and forth "let's talk" or "I miss you" for a month or two even though Cadence knew he was with Tiny. She hoped that he would leave her, but she quickly realized that he never had plans to. He wanted to have his cake and eat it too, and he was eating like a fat kid. Cadence made a declaration to herself that she was absolutely through playing games with Bo. She decided that she deserved better and she would not come second to anyone even though Bo tried to convince her she wasn't second she knew she wasn't receiving the time or respect she deserved.

Bo would call, but Cadence wouldn't pick up the phone. She knew he only wanted one thing! After a while Bo's calls started to diminish and Cadence began to feel a sense of relief.

Ignoring Bo was hard, but necessary for her to let him go! Out the blue Cadence looked down at her cell phone and saw Bo's name. She answered the phone in an annoyed voice

"Hello", but what Cadence heard on the other line was a shock to her life.

The voice on the other line softly spoke "Hello this is Tiny." Cadence's mouth dropped, and the drama began.

Khalil felt like he was living the American Dream. He was at the courts daily, doing what he loved playing basketball and making money hustling while doing it! It had to be the best of both worlds.

He was still trying to find a way to fully recover from the financial & emotional loss of Kenneth and Kane.

The funeral was approaching on Friday and he knew that the emotional stress was about to resurface like never before. He would have to deal with the pain in a double dosage since Kenneth and Kane were having their funeral together. The family had decided they only wanted to take the harsh blow once, and felt like this was the best way to deal with the tragedy on this level.

Khalil was on edge all week at the courts which was trouble for anyone who wasn't a part of the Dirty Dozen. He wasn't a bully, but his tolerance was extremely low when faced with a lot of stress.

Mikey knew Khalil was dealing with a lot and tried to comfort his friend.

Mikey said "Khalil isn't it time to do something different. It's more to life than the block and these courts. I have a game at YMCA this Saturday. Why don't you come? I'll pick you up at noon."

Khalil thought about it. He knew he had the funeral on Friday and he didn't know what would come with that! All he knew was that he felt the need for something different. Life was beginning to become mundane. He was getting bored with the same ole women, the block, and even his court.

He thought to himself "I'm sure it couldn't be that bad." Khalil told Mikey "I'm there it ain't nothing else to do anyway."

They decided to leave the courts early to smoke and relieve the stress of the upcoming days and hit up a few of the courts where the other Dirty Dozen members were.

The week seemed to fly past, and before Khalil knew it the funeral had approached. It was Friday morning and Khalil regrettably put on his Rest In Peace shirt and made his way outside to catch a ride to the funeral.

Mikey decided to take Khalil, because he knew he needed support. They picked up Cheese and Ralph and were on their way.

When they arrived at the funeral home everyone looked extremely drained. They had been crying for so long it seemed as if no one had any tears left. Everyone represented in their shirts with their favorite pictures of Kenneth and Kane as Khalil observantly sat in the back alone trying to figure out how life came to this.

Khalil put his head in his lap, because he couldn't stand the sight of the double caskets any longer. He quietly wept, and then looked up as he felt someone's presence next to him.

When he looked up he saw Tommy. Tommy was a very soft spoken guy from the hood. He was very watchful and never really conversed with Khalil much. He was short and brown skin, and extremely humble. You wouldn't know that Tommy was a money maker unless you really "knew" Tommy. He wasn't a flashy type of guy he just wanted to fly under the radar. He kept himself that way, because people had tried to rob him in the past and he quickly realized that the less people knew about you the less they would come after you.

Khalil was younger than Tommy, but knew exactly who he was. He was Kenneth and Kane's right hand man, but Khalil questioned why he was sitting next to him.

Tommy looked as if he had been drinking since he received the phone call although he was sober minded he was extremely hurt.

Tommy started to speak "What's up Khalil?"

Khalil shrugged his shoulders and softly replied "I can't call it Tommy. I can't call it!" Tommy choked back the tears "Me either! This just don't seem real."

Khalil shook his head and could only manage to respond "Man."

Tommy continued "This may not be the best time, but I wanted to holla at you about something."

Khalil nodded as to give him the consent to continue.

Tommy continued "You know those were my mans. I don't know if you know how involved I was, because I am a background type of dude, but I was in it in it. If you know what I mean."

Khalil took that in for a moment he actually was a bit shocked, but as he started to replay situations in his mind he remembered conversations with Kenneth and Kane where they were telling him without telling him. Khalil nodded as he made sure he didn't talk prematurely.

Tommy continued "Everything that was done was a three way split. We were equal partners. Kenneth and Kane raved about you before their death, and I trust them with my life."

Khalil nodded again. The wheels in Khalil's head began to turn and he was starting to wonder where Tommy was going with this.

Tommy took a deep breath trying to keep his composure as the funeral of his two best friends was proceeding right before his eyes. "You know Kenneth and Kane left to re-up, but they only took half of the money with them. They left the other half with me and I was supposed to wire it to the connect."

Khalil looked in disbelief Kenneth and Kane were still making power moves in their death.

"They called me before they boarded the plane, and told me they shipped half of the product through the mail and when they returned home I could wire the rest of the money when they got back."

"So I basically have money and a product that NO ONE knows about!" "I know you gave them money! I'm not sure how much, because they never said, but I just wanted to let you know I got you! We can chop up the details after all of the smoke from this clears, but take my word for it bro! I got you!"

Khalil sat there amazed! He was so worried about how things would work out, and there was finally light at the end of the tunnel. Khalil knew of Tommy, but didn't know him that well. He believed him, but he took his words with a grain of salt, and as quickly as Tommy appeared he disappeared.

Khalil sat there alone thinking "If bro keeps his word it's on!" He looked to the front of the church and remembered he was at the double funeral of two of his life lines and it all began to sink in again. He sat there alone thinking how quickly life could flash before your eyes, and he promised himself from that moment on to live everyday like it was his last.

Chapter 4

Cadence was extremely happy that the Friday night horror had ended. As she laid in the bed early Saturday morning she replayed the call with Tiny in her head. She remembered Tiny's soft spoken voice asking to speak to her. She obliged, rhetorically asking "Who is this?" Cadence very well knew who it was, but couldn't give Tiny the satisfaction.

Tiny replied this is "Tiny Bo's woman very sternly."

Cadence could remember the steam that was beginning to emit from her head. She tried to cool herself down to have a civil conversation.

"Yeah what's up?'

Tiny continued "I just wanna know what's going on with you and Bo. You constantly call him all hours of the night, you text him, and ask him to come see you. I think it's pathetic especially when someone is telling you they don't want you! When he's telling you he wants me, and I'm the one for him!

Tiny was about to continue but couldn't because Cadence abruptly erupted in a soul shaking laughter. Cadence could feel how pissed Tiny was.

Tiny asked angrily "What's so funny Cadence?"

Cadence tried to control her laughter before she began, but she couldn't help the occasional chuckles.

"Listen here Tiny I don't know you and quite frankly I don't care to know you, but what I do know is that Bo is a two-timing liar. He has NEVER fixed his lips to begin to tell me anything of the sort. With that being said you can have him anyway, because anybody who takes the time to clean out a syrup bottle to drink water out of in the middle of the night is just way beneath me!"

Tiny paused for a moment and then Cadence heard the dial tone.

Cadence sat up in her bed feeling a little sad, because she had exaggerated a bit. Bo did tell her he wanted to be with Tiny, not as detailed as he had explained to Tiny, but he did mention it, but she couldn't let her have the satisfaction.

Cadence thought "Well today is a new day, and anyway it's time to hit the gym." Something about the gym and basketball took her mind away from the mess of her life. Cadence got up and got dressed. She felt exceptionally good for some reason so she put in a little extra effort with her appearance, and she was off to the gym for the day to blow off a little steam.

Khalil drunkenly woke up to the ringing of his cellphone. He looked at the time and it was 11:59 a.m. It was Mikey.

He groggily answered. "Hello."

Mikey yelled through the phone "Khalil wassup boy I'm outside I told you I had a game fam."

Khalil remembered he was supposed to hit the gym with Mikey today. He started to say just go without me.

Before he could start talking Mikey said "Come on boy I ain't taking no for an answer."

Khalil agreed he needed to do something to get his mind off of Kenneth and Kane anyway. He told Mikey to give him ten minutes so he could throw on some clothes. Mikey agreed and continued bumping his DMX as loud as possible outside of Khalil's apartment.

Khalil scuffled through the clothes that were spattered about the floor. He found yesterday's pants, and a t-shirt from the previous day. He threw it on. He ran into the washroom got a hot rag, and wiped his face. He felt so relieved it was if he had washed away some of the pain from yesterday with one swipe. Khalil brushed his teeth, and took a look in the full length mirror. He was feeling himself. Something that wasn't uncommon for Khalil.

Mikey smirked as he saw Khalil walking briskly to the car. Khalil opened the door and Mikey started.

"I know you ain't wash your butt that quick boy."

Khalil laughed "Naw."

Mikey began to drive and turned to Khalil and said "roll up".

Khalil looked perplexed "You're going to smoke before your game."

Mikey replied "I don't know no other way."

Khalil shrugged his shoulders and pulled a bag of dro from a slit he cut in his pants to keep his weed dipped." He proceeded to roll up as they drove to the gym getting lifted still bobbing their heads to DMX letting the music take them to another place.

Cadence arrived at the gym pumped to play ball. She walked in the door extremely happy in spite of yesterday's events. It was 15 min before the start of her game so she decided to proceed directly to the locker room. Cadence was becoming aware of herself.

She knew that if she went into that gym room first she would begin socializing and she would be late for the start of her game. Procrastination was an extreme problem of hers and she was diligently trying to work on it! In the locker room she began to change her pants to shorts, and put on her basketball shoes. As she was looking down tying her shoes she heard a familiar voice say

"Man Cadence are you good?'

Cadence looked up and saw K.

The last time she had seen K she knew K was trying to tell her something, but she was so intent on seeing Bo she had kinda brushed K off.

Cadence slowly replied "Man K I'm good! I'm sorry though! You were trying to tell me, and I was so delusional about Bo I couldn't even listen to you!"

K lowered her head a little and then said "Yeah I knew it was coming! One of the dudes in the crew had told me. I ain't wanna get all in ya'll business! I tried to tell you, but I wasn't going to press the issue too far either though."

Cadence replied "It's all good! You ready to play?"

K lit up like a light. Basketball was a very vital part of her life. K responded "Girl you know I am!

We play the Heat so this should be a good game. I'm about to shoot their lights out."

Cadence got up and stuffed her things into a locker and shut the door behind her. Both women proceeded to walk out of the locker room laughing and chuckling along the way. They entered the gym room just before the start of their games and parted ways.

K told Cadence "good luck."

Cadence responded "Yeah you too! See you after the games."

Mikey and Khalil pulled up to the gym with a cloud of thick smoke following them like a shadow. They opened the doors of the car to exit, and smoke escaped as if they were exiting a sauna.

Khalil looked at Mikey and said "Aye you don't think they will trip about us smelling like this?"

Mikey chuckled in response "smelling like what he asked smirking with a huge bottle of Ozium in his hand."

This was a sure fire hood way to get rid of any smell from two week old garbage, to fish, and even the infamous weed smell. Mikey sprayed the Ozium on himself as he twirled in circles like an amateur male ballerina.

Khalil looked intently partially because he was so high, and also because he couldn't believe that Mikey opted to douse himself with the Ozium in that manner.

Mikey felt the intenseness of Khalil's stare and manned up saying "What?" as roughly as he could muster up without laughing.

He passed Khalil the bottle and Khalil looked at Mikey as if to say this is how you do it.

Khalil proceeded to spray the Ozium in the air thickly and walked back and forth through it.

Mikey nodded to accept the new way to "freshen up."

They sprayed the car, grabbed their bags and walked into the gym. By this time the gym was packed with adults who had a love for basketball. They had all paid to sign up for these adult leagues so there was a serious competition ensuing.

Khalil looked around astonished that so many people came here to play ball. He saw a few people he knew and began to get happy that he came. Mikey told Khalil that his game didn't start for another hour or so. They decided to chill and watch a few games before he started.

Cadence and K had just finished playing and were at the end of the last court debriefing about the game.

Mikey saw them from a distance and his wheels started turning again. He remembered what happened between Cadence and Bo and he vowed to himself to make it better for her.

What better way he thought then to introduce her and Khalil. Khalil sat there obviously watching the games really into it. He loved the game of basketball, and had a very high basketball IQ.

Mikey turned to Khalil and said "Hey bro let's go down here for a minute."

Khalil followed looking at all the games on his way.

Mikey "accidently" bumped into Cadence and K.

Mikey started to talk "What's up y'all?" "What did yall do in the game?"

K started first she was extremely excited "I was killing G, she began. I had 15 points and 5 assists."

Mikey replied "Dang, you was killing! Did y'all win?"

K smirked "Now you know we won."

Mikey turned to Cadence.

Cadence replied "same ole same ole."

Cadence wasn't as great a ball player as K. She was good defensively, but her offense came in spurts, but she loved the game so it kept her playing.

Cadence continued "we won though."

Mikey smiled "That's what's up y'all."

Khalil was standing a little away from their conversation; he wasn't paying any attention at all to what was going on. He was too busy watching the game.

Mikey said "Khalil."

Khalil woke up from his basketball trance and stepped forward to the group.

Mikey continued "Khalil this is K pointing to his right, and this is Cadence pointing to his left."

Khalil nodded, and began to look intently with a bit of confusion.

Mikey continued "K and Cadence this is Khalil."

Both of the women smiled and said hello.

After the pleasantries there was a long awkward silence, and finally K said it's a good game on court one let's go watch.

Before they could get too far Khalil erupted in laughter! "It's you! Clumsy Baby Girl that flipped me the bird!"

Cadence turned around and looked hard. She was a bit taken aback, but as she looked at him longer she remembered. He was the man from Bo's block that she had ran into that day trying to summon her Uber!

Cadence rolled her eyes and replied "I'm not clumsy and my name ain't baby girl it's Cadence!" She could feel herself getting butterflies. Dude was fine.

Khalil replied "Whatever!" As he flashed a million dollar smile giving Cadence the same reply she had given him weeks prior.

K and Cadence talked about the guys on their way to the first court.

K began "Who was dude?"

Cadence replied "I don't know. One day when I was leaving Bo's house I was pissed, because some bitch showed up. I left his crib trying to get an Uber and literally ran into dude and hit the ground! He helped me up but told me some shit like "To be aware is to be alive! I just "Whatevered" his ass, and kept it moving!"

K continued "He had swag."

Cadence agreed, and added "He was fine too!"

The women chuckled like school girls and thought nothing else of it.

Mikey and Khalil stood there beginning their conversation about the girls.

Mikey started "So what do you think?"

Khalil replied confused "Think about what?"

Mikey replied about "K and Cadence?"

Khalil stared blankly. "I saw Cadence on the block one day. She walked right into me and fell! I tried to help her up, but she had a bad ass attitude and "Whatevered me!" "She's fine though!" "What's to them?"

Mikey said "I've known them forever they're some good women, some really good women."

Khalil shrugged his shoulders and said "Oh" and continued to watch the games thinking nothing else of it!

Chapter 5

Life seemed to be back on track for Cadence. Work was going great! She was on her way to being a partner at the firm. She had gotten rid of that sorry ass boy of a man Bo, and she was keeping herself busy working out and playing ball. What more could she ask for?

As she drove on her way to hoop Cadence had a permanent smile on her face, and couldn't imagine life getting any better. Cadence had been spending most of her time there. Her basketball team had been winning like crazy, and things seemed to be at an all-time high.

During her constant days at the gym she noticed that Mikey and his friend had been there more frequently. They always seemed to be in the same area as her and K, pleasantries would be exchanged, but things just seemed a bit weird. As she thought about it more she realized how weird K acted when Mikey's friend was around.

A light bulb went off in Cadences' head. "OMG!" Cadence said to herself.

"K thinks she's slick. I bet she likes Khalil."

Cadence chuckled.

Cadence knew how selective K was about her personal business.

She was very quiet and although they were friends she never said much about anything. It was just K's way of protecting herself.

Cadence thought "When I get to the gym I'm asking K about it I know I ain't crazy." Cadence continued her drive to the gym blasting her music out the windows and enjoying her view. She was amazed at how she had come out of that period of life with just a few emotional bruises.

Cadence had a feeling that something was working on her behalf, but she had no idea what it was. She brushed it off, and parked her car in the parking lot of the YMCA.

Upon walking into the gym Cadence saw K in the corner smiling from ear to ear. Now smiling wasn't an unusual thing for K it actually was very common, but the depth of this smile reminded you of the humongous Kool-Aid pitcher from the commercials.

Cadence couldn't quite see who K was talking to because her view was obstructed so she kept walking down the path to the gym. When Cadence entered the gym she heard a familiar voice holler.

"Hey, Cadence over here."

Cadence turned her head in the direction of the voice and saw Mikey smiley crookedly.

"What's up Mikey?" Cadence said as she proceeded to walk in his direction.

Mikey smirked "Nothing, what's good?"

Cadence replied "You tell me! All of a sudden you are a gym super-star." "You are here every day now with your buddy. What's with that?" "And speaking of your buddy where is he? "You left him on the block today huh?"

Mikey looked angrily at Cadence and then softened up laughing "What makes you think he comes from the block Cadence, and how do you know he's not here?"

Cadence looked around the gym intently with her hand on her forehead like she was saluting a soldier while searching for a lost treasure, a gesture that was mostly exaggerated to mess with Mikey.

"I don't see him, and I know he's from the block, because he breathes the block. You can tell by the way he walks, talks, and how guarded he is. Not to mention I saw him out there sitting on a mailbox! You gotta be pretty damn comfortable to sit outside on the mailbox!"

Mikey gave Cadence a look of approval and said "He's here somewhere. Last time I saw him he was" before Mikey could continue his sentence K and Khalil entered the gym laughing hysterically.

Cadence looked perplexed and Mikey returned the exchange. The two walked over to their friends and both said

"What's up?"

Their question was followed by a long awkward silence.

Cadence started to speak slowly saying "Well, K I need to go put on my stuff come to the locker room with me."

K obliged and they walked off. Walking to the locker room K could feel the conversation coming on so she proceeded to spill the beans.

"I've been talking to Khalil for a couple weeks now and I really really like him." "He is funny, smart, and super cool." "He's like the male me."

Cadence took a deep breath "Girl I knew I wasn't crazy." "She laughed. I'm happy for you! He seems like a pretty cool dude."

Yeah he is, K replied. "I talk to him all the time. I think he might be the one."

Cadence looked perplexed "The one for what?"

K just looked begrudgingly.

Cadence lowered her head in acceptance of her submission and continued to get dressed with the absence of words from either of them.

Khalil was finally back on the right track. It had been a couple of weeks since the double funeral, and things were beginning to be slightly normal again. He had been spending a lot of time at the gym, but He still missed his guys very much! He knew that Kenneth and Kane would want for him to get some money in the sake of their name so he did.

Tommy came through and laid out the terms of their agreement. One late night when Khalil was sitting on the block Tommy pulled up on his way going in. He saw Khalil and called him over to his all black Jeep 4X4. Khalil hopped in.

Tommy said "Let's ride."

Khalil nodded, and Tommy headed toward north Lake Shore Drive.

Tommy began, "I got everything in order Khalil." "Are you ready to roll?"

Khalil nodded his head.

Tommy told Khalil "I have 100 pounds of weed and 3 bricks for you!"

Khalil started to calculate the money in his mind. He couldn't help it, that's just how his brain worked.

Tommy continued "I'm going to give you a deal so you can get your money back up." "It's more about the relationship building and getting rid of the product for me." "Just give me 30,000 for everything this go round."

Khalil looked in astonishment. That was more than a deal in his mind it was like hitting a stain. Khalil slightly lifted his body out of the passenger seat and dug in his pocket. He counted out $5,000 dollars in a mixture of hundreds, fifties, twenties, fives, and singles leaving himself six dollars to his name.

He placed the money next to the car's gear shift and looked at Tommy confidently saying "I'm more than ready to roll."

Tommy was taken aback by the tenacity that he possessed and he knew this match was going to build a friendship, but most importantly it was going to make a lot of money.

Khalil hopped out the car and entered his apartment waiting for sunrise. Tommy said he would bring the product on the block today, and Khalil was ready to get to business.

Khalil was totally happy in the space he was in. He had a way to get money, he was hopping which was his second love, he had success with his crew, and he had a slew of women on his jock. He was living his best life.

Khalil also had a new chick from the gym that he added to his posse. He actually liked the girl. He thought about how she was super cool. She was funny, smart, loved basketball, and had swag. She reminded him of him in a female version. He never went to the gym with women on his mind, but he definitely had no problem pulling them wherever he went. He had enough women to juggle, but K came with a whole bunch of friends which was always beneficial.

Khalil usually only messed with women who ran in a small crew of some sort. Khalil needed women who had friends to fulfill the needs of his crew.

K was the perfect candidate.

She had so many friends it was hard to keep up with it. She was just a charismatic outgoing girl and people loved her. Not to mention she was hilariously funny. Khalil and K were a good little match for the time being.

They both served a purpose for each other Khalil thought to himself.

It was good while it was going. Khalil went to the bathroom to brush his teeth. He looked in the mirror and saw his father for a second. He missed Kaleb. Phone calls weren't enough; he needed him there to navigate through life, but Khalil threw water in his face and brushed it off like he did everything else. He grabbed his gym bag and his army green bomber jacket, and slammed the front door behind him.

When he reached the morning sun Mikey was sitting in front of the house with his usual cloud of smoke emitting from his car. Khalil opened the door and hopped in.

He smiled cunningly and said "What's the plan for today?"

Mikey accordingly responded "We are about to take over the world?"

They both laughed and proceeded to the courts to put their Pinky and The Brain plan in motion.

When they arrived at Hayes the Dirty Dozen was waiting in the parking lot. The crew had grown so immensely that Khalil felt like there were way too many people to keep a handle on, but Mikey kept assuring him that it was cool.

Khalil, Mikey and the crew had mastered the art of swerving their females during their time at the courts. They had so many women that they were actually engaged in "relationships' ' with and then so many more on their heels that they just made it known that there would be NO public displays of affection. It was a Dirty Dozen rule to never commit to any one female. It was the one of the fore founding bylaws. It helped to keep them out of the female drama circuit, and keep all of their girls committed to their cause.

The courts were amazing for Khalil today! Crews were coming from all sides of town to play for money, but Khalil's mind was elsewhere. Yeah he made money on the courts, but Khalil was ready to get to the block and get the work from Tommy! That was the most important thing to him. He knew he had to take care of business, and he had a lifestyle to uphold. It wasn't every day that you saw a man of his demeanor so fly in a black pair of Amiri jeans, A black Chrome Hearts shirt with white writing, Louie shoes and a Louie Belt, with a couple of chains to add accent, and an army green bomber jacket, but most importantly a charisma out of this world all on his own account.

He knew what he had to do, and the reality of the matter was that Khalil had the mindset to do anything to get ahead there were no limits, and so it began.

Chapter 6

Cadence was becoming friends with an unusual suspect: Khalil.

Since Cadence and K were such close friends it was just natural for Khalil and Cadence to always be around each other

. They instantly clicked and became friends.

Khalil and Cadence talked everyday about everything. Their friendship was growing everyday more and more.

Khalil and Cadence would talk for hours about everything under the sun from K, to basketball, to life, to his other females, politics or whatever.

There were no boundaries with Khalil and Cadence!

They talked about it all!

Cadence felt like she had found a new best friend.

Cadence would seek out Khalil for advice about dudes, and he always kept it real, holding nothing back at all.

He became her only male ally. Lastly, adding the most unexpected addition to her list of close circuit friends that she was composing was........ Tiny. Yes, Tiny!

They had something in common; a disgust for Bo.

Bo began to play games with Tiny and she knew the drill.

She was quick to drop dudes like a bad habit. She slowly moved herself away from Bo as he began to start entertaining another girl.

Tiny called Cadence and asked for some advice on a situation, and the friendship began to flourish from there.

Tiny was actually a very cool girl.

She was absolutely hilarious, a trait that her and Cadence shared so there was never a dull moment between the two.

Jokes seemed to flow like water when they were together.

Cadence knew it was a little weird for her to be friends with Tiny, but she felt like why should she be mad at her. Tiny wasn't in a relationship with her, Bo was. .

Tiny was fun! She was always on the go. She knew people everywhere, and she was always ready for the party. Tiny actually was becoming an intricate part of Cadence's little crew. Things were seeming to come together and Cadence was at a place of peace. A place that she hasn't resided in for a long time.

Khalil was back on.

He was getting money like never before.

Tommy had put Khalil and the Dream Team in the position to see more money than they had ever seen before.

Khalil was now spending more time on the block, because he had work to do.

He knew the importance of making money.

Money was Khalil's lifeline and without it he felt as if he would die.

The courts began to take a toll on Khalil, because it was no longer his primary focus.

If it wasn't about the money Khalil really didn't want any part of it.

Khalil's mother began to notice a shift in Khalil's demeanor, and his lack of enthusiasm pertaining to hooping which she knew was his first love.

She decided that it would be a great time to approach Khalil and see what was going on. Nadine drove Khalil's apartment late on Saturday night, and got the shock of her life.

Khalil had just finished coming from "the store". His apartment was filled with drug paraphernalia.

There were small scales, red box baggies, earring bags, razor blades, scissors, and Ozium!

Nadine was in complete shock! She wasn't oblivious to the game.

She knew it very well from all her time spent with Kaleb Khalil's dad.

She took a deep breath for a moment, because she was so angry at the fact that Khalil had chosen this lifestyle.

She wanted to kill him, but what could she expect?

She began to blame herself for all of Khalil's shortcomings.

She blamed herself for having babies by Kaleb.

She blamed herself for exposing Khalil to that environment for so long.

She blamed herself for moving to the neighborhood.

She had a plethora of thoughts running through her head a million miles per hour.

She finally popped Khalil in the back of his head as he peacefully slept on his mattress fully clothed including shoes.

Khalil popped up quickly as if he heard gunshots, and was prepared for war.

When he saw that it was Nadine he calmed down tremendously and said "What's up Ma?" groggily as he tried to wake up.

It took only a few moments for him to realize that Nadine was in his apartment!

The apartment that he failed to clean because he was extremely exhausted from the overtime he was putting in on the block.

He jumped up quickly and began to start expeditiously grabbing all of the inappropriate things within his reach.

Nadine watched him fumble for a moment, and then gently grabbed his hands and softly said "Khalil we need to talk."

Khalil's heart sunk to his feet not because Nadine found the things in his apartment, but because he disappointed her.

Khalil never wanted to disappoint Nadine.

She was the most important person in his life.

She stuck by him when no one else would.

When Kaleb was absent: there was Nadine.

When his friends disappeared: there was Nadine.

When the girls left: there was Nadine, and when the money was all gone: There was always Nadine.

He couldn't begin to phantom what was about to come out of Nadine's mouth, but he knew it wouldn't be good.

He braced himself trying to hold back the tears from the thought of hurting the only person he knew for sure loved him unconditionally.

Nadine dropped her head and began "Khalil, I always wanted more out of life for you. I explained to you the repercussions of this lifestyle on a daily basis. You have seen firsthand what this lifestyle gets you. Where is Kaleb? In jail! He has been there off and on your whole life! Is that the type of life you want for yourself?

Khalil was about to answer the question, but was cut off by Nadine as she continued.

"You are talented beyond belief. You could do and be anything you put your mind to Khalil, but yet you choose to focus on this!"

"You know that you can't live right conducting your life in this manner, right?"

Khalil didn't know if it was his turn to speak or not.

He slowly began to open his mouth and stumble over his words. "M....Ma, I just wanted to get some money. I saw how you were struggling to take care yourself, and you're helping take care of my nieces and nephews so I wanted to make your burden lighter. I know it is wrong, but I was only going to do it for a little while until I got myself together."

Nadine put up her hand in a stop motion as to tell Khalil to be quiet.

Khalil conceded and closed his mouth.

Nadine began "Khalil this is a very dangerous game. There is no getting yourself together or getting out scot free. This game comes with consequences and repercussions. You may be able to get in the game easy, but getting out is another story. There are usually only two ways out: jail or the grave. Very few walk away from this untouched! The deeper you get in the harder it is to get out! The more money you make the more addicted you become to the lifestyle, and the more money you spend. It's a vicious cycle that never ends! You need to make some life altering decisions Khalil, because you are playing rush and roulette with your life with a loaded gun!"

Khalil just sat there in disbelief.

He knew that Nadine had to know something being with his father for so many years she was fully versed in the game and it was shocking to him.

Nadine turned around to exit Khalil's apartment and looked back momentarily and told Khalil "Choose wisely?"

Khalil began to think about the things that Nadine was saying to him. "Choose wisely." Resonated in Khalil's spirit the look on Nadine's face and her tone of voice made it so real for him.

He sat on the edge of the bed thinking of all the things he could be doing other than the drug game.

He could be playing basketball, and prepping himself for the NBA.

He could be a mentor, or play baseball, or even chess he was smart beyond belief.

So why did he choose this lifestyle he thought to himself.

As he was deep in thought his phone began to ring.

He looked down at the screen and saw that it was Ralph so he flipped the top of his phone to answer, and sadly said "Yeah Ralph what's to it?"

Ralph replied "Ole boy off 75th wants 6 Bo's. He's about to slide on you right now!"

Khalil quickly remembered why he chose the life he did.

He didn't know anyone else who could make $6,000 from one phone call!

He grabbed his keys, copped the 6 Bo's stuffed them in a bookbag, and ran quickly out the apartment door. He hoped Nadine was long gone from his apartment, because he knew what he needed to do.

Chapter 7

Cadence was enjoying her new found friendships.

It gave her something to do other than work and the basketball league.

She began to hang out more as this wasn't a common thing for her.

What was even more uncommon was the fact that when you saw Cadence that Tiny wasn't too far in tow.

It seemed as if her circle had drastically changed.

She was always with Tiny!

Or Cadence was spending time with Khalil.

The friendship was a bit awkward at first, but they had become best friends.

Cadence and Khalil began to see each other outside of the basketball league at the Y, and outside of K.

Cadence felt a little bad about the situation although the friendship she had with K was sort of parting ways.

She also knew firsthand of how Khalil really felt, but she knew it still wasn't right, but she couldn't help it.

She felt like her and Khalil had some sort of bond that couldn't be broken.

Cadence would find herself kicking it on the block with Khalil and his friends.

Of course, she would bring Tiny along.

The friendship that she had with Khalil started to transform into something more right before her eyes.

One day Cadence had decided to leave work early and go home.

On her way to the house she received a phone call from Khalil.

She smiled and answered the phone.

Khalil asked what she was doing, and she replied on my way home from work.

Khalil said "I'll meet you at your house."

Cadence replied "Okay I'll be there in 15 minutes."

When Cadence was pulling up the block Khalil was pulling up with Mikey.

Mikey nodded and smiled as he thought to himself that his plan finally panned out. Cadence smiled and waved and thought nothing of Khalil coming over.

He had been over plenty of times before.

She would cook and they would chill and watch TV.

However, today would be something totally different.

Khalil hopped out the car and said to Cadence slyly "What's up girl? What you about to cook me?"

Cadence laughed "Why are you ALWAYS hungry when you come over here? Why didn't you bring us something to eat?"

Khalil looked perplexed and then responded. "I'm tired of eating fast food. I eat it all day every day. I need some real food."

Cadence looked at Khalil and responded "Whatever boy."

Cadence stuck her key into the first door, and they both began to walk up the stairs. The got to the second door and Cadence began to unlock the lock, and then the door.

She felt an odd aura between them and as she got the door open she turned around to Khalil and looked him in the eyes and said "What's up with you?"

Khalil walked toward Cadence and whispered "I ain't come over here for no food Cadence. I came over here for you! He closed his eyes and backed Cadence to the mirror and began to kiss her.

Cadence was taken aback for a moment, but she knew she wanted Khalil also.

She wrapped her arms around his shoulders and began to kiss him back. Cadence was in a whirlwind of emotions as the kissing led to something more serious, and she found herself getting out of bed with Khalil and going to use the washroom.

She looked at herself in the mirror and couldn't believe what she had just done. Knowing that Khalil had so many girls flocking all over him, knowing that he never really cares about anyone, and fearing that she would be just another notch on his belt.

As Cadence thought about this all she wanted to begin to cry.

As soon as the tears started to form she heard a familiar voice "Cadence, what are you doing come here."

So lost in her emotions she almost forgot Khalil was still laying in her bed.

She slowly walked back to her room, and Khalil instantly knew something was wrong with her.

Khalil slowly said "Come here Cadence lay down."

Cadence slowly walked over to her bed and sat on the edge.

Khalil gently touched her back and said "What's wrong?"

Cadence replied "I know all about you, and what you do. I just made myself another notch on your belt, and that was never my intention. I never wanted to be one of many."

Khalil looked crazily at Cadence and said "This ain't that shorty. You ain't got nothing to worry about. Just be cool."

Khalil then proceeded to grab Cadence and lay her back down on the bed with him to continue what they started.

Cadence felt more at ease as if maybe Khalil really did care about her. She let go of the negative feelings and continued to embark on what she felt like was the beginning of her new life.

After they finished Cadence turned around and looked Khalil in the face.

Neither one of them said a word.

Khalil closed his eyes and fell asleep holding Cadence.

Cadence just knew this had to be love!

She turned around and watched television until she dozed off.

After an hour or so Khalil woke up and nudged Cadence jokingly saying "What's up with that food though?"

Cadence wiped her eyes and laughed. "You're a goofy. What do you want?"

Khalil left Cadence's house in astonishment.

He couldn't believe he finally went that far with her.

Mikey pulled up with his usual smoke cloud emitting from the car, and Khalil entered blank faced.

Mikey looked at Khalil and asked him "What's wrong?"

Khalil replied "Nothing man! I just went there with Cadence, and I don't know what to think about it."

Mikey asked perplexed "Went where?"

After a moment he realized how dumb his question was, and he chuckled "Oh!" Mikey proceeded "So what's the problem? Didn't you want to hit that?"

Khalil was taken aback by the question Mikey presented.

Khalil thought about the numerous conversations they had about the girls that they smashed in the past, but this felt slightly different. He really didn't view Cadence as "hitting it." He felt something stir up that he never felt before. He questioned himself "What is this?" He decided that he didn't have the time or energy to put into figuring it out. Instead he brushed it off and told Mikey to pass the blunt.

Mikey was still stuck on the conversation "Didn't you want to hit that?"

Khalil just conceded and said "Yeah I wanted to hit it, and I did!"

He felt awkward, but he let it go and rode to the block listening to Warren G and Nate Dog "Regulate", and smoking on the already lit doobie Mikey had in the air.

Khalil's mind began to shift to the money that needed to be made.

With each inhale he took he exhaled the thought of his encounter with Cadence.

He had to stay focused on the money.

He couldn't allow any outside forces to take him off his course.

He felt a vibration in his pocket.

He pulled out his phone and saw Cadence's number flashing across the screen.

Khalil stared at the phone for a minute.

He wanted to pick up, but he couldn't.

He had a feeling something was about to change, but he didn't know when or how.

He put his phone back into his pocket and got back into the zone.

As they cruised down lakeshore Khalil thought about all the things that needed to be done with the Dream Team on the block, and Cadence became a distant memory.

Chapter 8

Cadence felt a bit awkward after her encounter with Khalil.

He was the second person she had been with in her whole life and it was special to her, but when she called Khalil he began to pick up less and less.

She wondered what she had done wrong, but she brushed it off.

She had an entire life ahead of her and couldn't worry about a nigga! "Either we is or we ain't!" "I can't keep stressing!" She had things to do.

She was a top lawyer at a prestigious law firm and playing basketball.

Even though the situation with Khalil was crazy she kept on about her business.

Tiny and Cadence were thick as thieves. They would go everywhere and do everything. You could catch them at all the clubs turning up.

The issue for Cadence was that she would catch Khalil there too!

Cadence wasn't the type of girl to be all in Khalil's face she would do her.

It was a weekend at Club O, and Cadence ran into Khalil and his crew after not speaking to him for a week or so.

Cadence was at the party with Tiny and Mya, and saw Khalil as she entered.

Khalil saw Cadence and walked over and said "Cadence what's up?"

Cadence looked around as if to see if he was talking to her since he hadn't returned one of her calls in the last week or so.

Khalil whispered in her ear, because of the loud music "I'm sorry Cadence! I've been busy! I've been trying to get some money."

Cadence responded "So....you couldn't pick up the phone?"

Khalil looked away!

He knew he was lying.

He hadn't answered Cadence, because he didn't know what to say to her.

The dynamics of their relationship had changed, and he didn't know what to do.

He loved being her friend, and he knew how much of a "good girl" Cadence was!

He didn't want to take the chance of ruining her with his shitty ways.

He knew he wasn't ready to be in a relationship with Cadence, but he really needed her.

Every block boy needed a good girl, right? He thought to himself.

He couldn't pass up on Cadence.

He was taking his time to figure out what he wanted to do.

He had limited time to spend with her with all his responsibilities on the block, but he wanted to mold her to be what he needed her to be.

He was just taking the time to figure out if she was worth it.

He had figured it out and Cadence was definitely worth it!

He had to get back in her good graces though, and he knew a couple of laughs and an apology should do the trick.

He liked her and knew she at least deserved that.

What was even odder is Cadence was nothing like the girls Khalil was used to.

She was fully clothed, reserved, smart, and a complete lame.

Khalil usually dealt with the girls that were in it!

Cadence however put him in the mindset of Nadine, and he always tried to be steps ahead of the game.

Cadence was his plan for the future.

He tried to keep that in mind when dealing with her. With that in mind he began with his apology.

Cadence looked at Khalil and couldn't resist; He was stupid. Stupid in a funny way; he kept her laughing.

Their foundation for the friendship kept them strong in her eyes.

She felt like Khalil felt more for her than he said, but she could never quite put her finger on it. They made up, and went their separate ways in the party.

Cadence, Tiny, and Mya were kicking it hard. It was packed! Everybody was there this weekend and the hottest young DJ was killing it!

DJ Bman was like a young Chicago legend, and if he was playing the music you knew the party was going to be on point.

Cadence, Tiny, and Mya were doing their thang, and when they looked around Cadence saw a familiar face.

It was Cheese he was smiling from ear to ear as usual trying to shoot his shot at Tiny.

Cadence laughed hysterically in her head, because she just knew Tiny wouldn't give Cheese the time of day.

But contrary to what she thought Tiny began to exchange pleasantries.

Cadence was perplexed.

Cheese did have a little swag, but CHEESE Cadence thought.

Tiny continued to talk, Cadence slightly danced, and Mya watched, because dancing was NOT her thing unless she was drinking.

After cell phone numbers were exchanged Cheese walked away with the biggest smile Cadence had ever seen.

Tiny returned to her friends, and Cadence gave her the look.

Tiny said I know, but I think I like him. He's funny. Cadence chuckled and replied "Yeah I'll give you that!" The party continued to go on until........

Khalil hated the spotlight, but understood that if he tolerated disrespect on any level that the reputation of the Dirty Dozen and The Dream Team was on the line.

The party at Club O was on point until some dudes started acting crazy.

That was the thing about parties Khalil thought to himself.

All these different cliques something was bound to happen and it did.

Some random dude said something to a guy from the Dirty Dozen, and the party was sent up. The next thing Khalil knew he was punching someone in the face.

He looked to the right and Mikey was stomping some dude out.

Everyone in the Dirty Dozen was fighting.

By this time security was trying to break-up the fight.

The Dirty Dozen started to scramble like roaches; jail wasn't an option. Khalil ran to the car with Mikey full speed ahead. They did a check to make sure everybody was good, and got up out that jam.

On the way back to the block the conversation was crazy. Khalil and his boys discussed what happened in detail, getting excited about how they sent the party to the moon.

Mikey said "What they thought this was?"

The rest of the guys laughed as blunts began to rotate through the car, and drinks started to make their way around the car in a constant rotation.

Khalil got quiet for a moment, and then said "It's just the Dirty Dozen now! It's us against the world."

Khalil thought it made no sense to have the Dream Team and the Dirty Dozen so he combined the two and made what he believed to be an unstoppable force.

He got a rush from the fight.

He hated for people to talk mess, and not be able to back it up.

He also took note of who didn't show up to the brawl. He was so appalled by Cheese he replayed the situation in his mind. Cheese was nowhere to be found in the rumble, but when things were phasing down and chains were being snatched he was on the front lines. Cheese was kicking people from behind other people, and snatching chains and laughing like he had been participatory in the fight and not just a bystander.

Khalil despised a person with these characteristics, but Cheese? Was this just fluke timing? Was he SCARED? Khalil thought to himself "I CAN NOT be around somebody that's scared!" "They bleed like I bleed!" "Is Cheese cut from the same cloth?" "I know I've been grooming him, but dang?" As Khalil was having these thoughts in his mind he shook it off and remembered where he was.

He looked at Cheese while he was in his false glow and took note.

Note that he wasn't as real as he claimed, and this was the beginning of the BIG reveal!

The next morning Khalil replayed the events from yesterday in his mind.

The Dirty Dozen was in full effect with an extensive membership, but there was some faultiness with its founding members.

Cheese was a complete fake. He was not cut from the same cloth. He was scared; scared to fight; scared to get money; sacred to be who he was just plain scared.

Jabar was selfish beyond belief. He couldn't see the big picture if it was right in his face and said "THIS IS THE BIG PICTURE".

He wouldn't listen. He was young and dumb and letting the false fame get to his head.

Big Boy was changing. He was altering into someone Khalil didn't know. Maybe it was the streets getting to him, and then there was Mikey.

Mikey was with it. What you saw was what you got with him, and Ralph was in his own world. If you didn't bother Ralph he didn't bother you. But something was missing in Khalil's eyes.

He went to seek advice from his mentor Chance. Chance was the hood guru. He had a great head on his shoulders. He had been in the streets since 14 and it was all he knew. He was smart and avoided jail at all costs.

Khalil knew that he was going to start having to make some drastic changes within the crew, but he needed some sound advice. Khalil walked down the block in deep thought trying to figure out what was going on in his life. He turned into the mustard yellow court yard with 6 entrances.

It was the "spot" on the block. You could serve there, but still live there comfortably. Khalil proceeded to the second entrance and rang the top bell. He heard a familiar voice yell through the microphone "What up?"

Khalil smirked and nodded his head slightly "It's Khalil buzz me up bro!" The voice responded "Aight."

Khalil walked the spiral staircase with stained brown carpet all the way to the top floor.

He entered the open door, and Chance spoke "To what do I owe the pleasure?" Khalil responded "Stop it!"

Chance continued as he locked the front door. "I haven't seen you in days, what's good?"

Before Khalil could even speak Chance interrupted saying "It's some mess going on ain't it. It's written all over your face."

Khalil tried to do a quick self-evaluation.

He was trained to never let anyone see his emotions even if it was Chance.

Khalil began to speak "The guys aren't who they say they are and it's perplexing to me. I've been with these dudes for years, and every time I turn around people are showing me a sucker part of them that I didn't know existed. I ain't with the sucker movement, and it burns my blood to have those types of people around me. Faulty character traits are a serious pet peeve of mine."

Chance looked serious for a moment then laughed hysterically.

Khalil started to get a bit annoyed, and then Chance spoke.

"In life you are lucky to have two good people in your corner; your parents. That's it, and that's not always a given. You shouldn't expect anything else! The streets, these "so-called homies", the chicks, the "sisters", and "bros", are all an illusion. In the end it's you against the world period!

Khalil sat staring at Chance for what felt like an eternity.

He knew this part of the game, but was always into giving people the benefit of the doubt, but he had an odd feeling that if he didn't go with what he knew he would be in a very bad predicament before he knew it.

When Khalil was about to leave Chance chuckled. "Little bro, here's your 3.5 back!" Khalil looked perplexed.

How did he get his merch in the first place, and it was a 7 he thought to himself.

Khalil began to speak "3.5?" "I had a 7!"

Not when you snoozing responded Chance.

Khalil accepted his redirection and left with the 3.5 knowing he hadn't been fully aware in the past weeks.

It was a lesson learned as usual when you come in contact with Chance.

Chapter 9

The bond between Cadence and Khalil was growing like wildfire.

She was always there when he needed her, and it seemed as if that made him need her more. Cadence felt so comfortable with him.

He was everything that she had hoped for, but Khalil had an issue.

Khalil was afraid of commitment.

The only thing he could give his all to was the streets.

He was committed to getting money and any and everything came second to that!

Whatever could bring him closer to the money was what he was into.

Cadence started to feel like she was giving her all, and coming in second place every time.

The more she wanted to spend time with Khalil the more "busy" he became. He always had something to do, but when she called all she heard was laughter and games.

Cadence wondered why he always had time to kick it, but never made time for her.

But when Khalil finally made the time for Cadence it felt like heavenly bliss to her. The time they spent was completely euphoric.

Cadence and Khalil would laugh and crack jokes like stand- up comedians: there was never a dull moment.

Even though she was completely pissed with him she could not stay mad.

He would always do something to make her laugh or down play the situation and every time she would fall into his trap.

Khalil's trap was encompassing Cadence and she didn't even see it happening.

Cadence started to slack big time.

Work and basketball started to take a back seat to her relationship with Khalil.

Cadence was losing herself and gaining parts of Khalil. His ways slowly started to become her ways, his language was becoming her new lingo, and his lifestyle now started to include her. The square, book smart, nerd was becoming a street pharmacists assistant.

The "life" was exciting and she was just getting a taste of it!

Khalil was beginning to trust Cadence, and trust in the streets was more valuable than money. He couldn't trust anyone, but Cadence; She was becoming his lifeline!

Khalil was trying to fight off the connection with Cadence, but really needed her around.

When he was in a bind she was there, she was honest, forthright, and down for the cause. Had he met his Bonnie?

After Khalil's conversation with Chance he felt relieved and dumb at the same.

He knew for a fact that he shouldn't expect people to be honest and forthright.

He knew people wouldn't keep it 100 at all times, but what perplexed him the most was why had he let his guards down with the Dirty Dozen anyway?

Was it the time spent with them?

Was it because he thought he was molding them to be better generals, and he actually thought they were receiving and retaining the information?

Or was it that he was getting soft and side tracked?

Had he let this emotional relationship with Cadence start spilling over into the rest of his life? Khalil was a certified killer and had no time to deal with emotions.

Emotions got you killed, but he felt something for her.

Something he knew he needed to push away in order to keep the Dirty Dozen running effectively and keep the money rolling in.

Because at the end of the day all that mattered was the money.

Chance got Khalil together! He was back on track and he knew what he needed to do.

He had to keep Cadence at bay!

Khalil stared off into space and began to think that the relationship had to be over, and he needed to figure out how to break it to her.

He knew it would be too difficult, because whenever he looked at her he just could do no wrong to her. He thought maybe he should just start to ignore her, but as soon as he was coming to grips with his new reality the trap phone rang.

It was Mikey on the other line. Mikey started talking.

"Khalil, what's good bro?"

Khalil replied "Nothing my dude? What's to it?"

Mikey chuckled sinisterly and began "Well, I was with one of the booties that used to go to the catholic school. She gets around bro, so she knows all the pockets of dudes. She started spilling the business about those dudes we stomped out at the club the other night. They apparently got a little click. They call themselves 9339. They say they got the land sewed up from 93rd to 39th and are pissed that we embarrassed them like that! They mess with all the little booties that we mess with too! They act like they are ready to get into some action with us!"

The wheels in Khalil's head were turning.

He definitely didn't care about the booties.

Chicks come and go and he could get sex anywhere, but action!

"They want action?" Thought Khalil.

He smirked and began to speak on the phone.

"So Mikey, they want action? "I don't think they really want no action!" "I think they tryin to stunt for the booties and they gonna end up hurt behind it!" "These chicks ain't loyal at all!" "But we can definitely bump into them to see what's to it! You know we ain't ducking nothing but the pigs and bad barbers!"

Mikey chuckled heartily and said "You right bro! We'll see them when we see them!"

"I'm finna come scoop you now though!

"Cool" Khalil replied and ended the call.

As he was about to return to his thought-process the phone rang.

He saw the name CADENCE flash across the screen.

He knew he had to shake her, but he didn't know how.

He ended the call and proceeded to get dressed to dip with Mikey.

His phone vibrated again. "Dang" he said out loud.

I know Mikey didn't make it yet where he was around the corner.

He picked his phone up off the bed and read the screen. CADENCE.

He thought to himself "I can't keep playing with this girl she has me to tweaked."

He ignored her call again.

He threw the phone back on the bed and proceeded to look for his Girbaud jeans. They were the light denim wash with the black Velcro at the knee and at the ankle. When you undid the Velcro you saw GIRBAUD in bold gray letters.

His swag was impeccable.

As he searched through piles of clothes he heard his phone vibrate again.

"Man" he thought! I know that's Mikey this time!

He reached for the phone and glanced at the screen- CADENCE!

Why is she blowing me up? Khalil thought.

I ain't really got nothing to say to her!

He went to put his phone down and it vibrated again!

CADENCE. He ended the call.

CADENCE. HE ended again!

CADENCE. Finally he answered.

"WHAT DO YOU WANT, QUIT CALLING MY PHONE MAN!!!

Cadence softly spoke. "I need to talk to you!"

Khalil replied "Ain't nothing to say! Beat it! Kick Rocks! Get on!"

Cadence took a deep breath to help her not begin to cry "I think I'm pregnant!!!!".

Khalil dropped his head, took a deep breath, and ended the call.

Chapter 10

PREGNANT! PREGNANT! Khalil thought.

I can't believe this! Khalil took a deep breath.

The gears in his mind started to rotate. He began to think how he could get out of this situation. He knew that he didn't want or need a baby right now.

He knew he couldn't afford to take care of a baby either.

He had the money, but wasn't ready to spend it like that!

Could I blame it on her? He thought.

I could say it wasn't my baby! Then Khalil shook his head.

I can't say that! Shorty ain't a bust-down.

Man! Khalil continued the conversation with himself for what felt like an hour.

He went back and forth over ways to get out of this jam.

It wasn't because Khalil was a bad dude, but because he understood the responsibility behind having children. He'd been helping raise his nieces and nephews since they had been born. He wasn't ready for a baby of his own.

"Just when I was about to separate myself from shorty: Now this!" thought Khalil.

Mikey was still on his way to pick Khalil up, but with the new found information he wasn't feeling like kicking it at all.

He really just wanted to smoke and clear his mind. He couldn't smoke at Nadine's crib so he found his clothes, grabbed his phone, and rushed toward the front door.

Mid-stride Khalil heard Nadine from the back room.

"Khalil" Nadine loving called out to him

. "Yeah Ma." Khalil replied.

Nadine asked him to come in the back.

Khalil was frustrated and needed to get out of her house badly, but it wasn't his mother's fault. Nadine loved him deeply and he respected her.

Khalil tried to fix his face.

Nadine was a master at reading people, a skill he picked up from her.

He pulled himself together and faked a smile.

He walked into the threshold of her doorway and said "What's up, Mama?"

Nadine looked Khalil over. She thought in her head "I love my son! If only he could live righteously".

As she was looking him over she sensed that something was wrong. His body language seemed a little off to her. She began to open her mouth to speak, but heard a buzzing sound.

Khalil reached for his pocket and looked at the screen of his phone: CADENCE.

He fumbled with the phone and quickly ended the call. He kept his head down for a moment and returned his phone to his pocket

. Nadine proceeded "Khalil what's going on with you?" she asked lovingly.

Khalil hated lying to his mother, but he knew he couldn't tell her about Cadence and the baby. Nadine believed in right is right and wrong is wrong. She would be sure to make Cadence have the baby.

Khalil replied "Nothing!" Nadine knew he wasn't being truthful. She wanted to press the issue. "Buzz" Khalil reached for his pocket again. He looked down at the screen: CADENCE! He decided to keep his phone in his hand.

Nadine looked at him and looked at his phone. "Khalil are you sure you are okay?" Nadine said. "Buzz" CADENCE; end call. "Buzz" CADENCE; end call. "Buzz" CADENCE; end call.

Khalil looked at his mother worn down from the stress and said "Ma it's more than one person should handle, but I got it! I'm going to make it right!

"Buzz" MIKEY.

Khalil sighed a breath of relief "Yo Mikey where you at wit it!" Khalil said.

Mikey replied "I'm outside my dude." Khalil looked at his mom.

"Don't worry I got this Ma! I gotta go Mikey is outside."

Nadine looked worried.

Khalil attempted to soothe her "Ma it ain't nothing bad at all! It's all good Ma! I got it."

Khalil walked over to his mother and kissed her on the cheek.

"See you later!"

Nadine didn't want Khalil to go, but asking him to stay in was redundant.

She watched him turn to walk away and said "Khalil make good choices!"

Khalil nodded respectfully and proceeded toward the front door.

He walked down the stairs and out the door.

The brisk breeze from off the lake slapped him in the face.

Relieved to be out of the house he thought "What's a good decision in this situation?"

He walked down the sidewalk toward the car. Once he reached the door he smelled the loud and got into mode. He was in the streets now, and Cadence and that situation had no place there.

He pushed it out his mind and hopped in the car. "Let me hit that blunt boy." Khalil said to Mikey.

Mikey passed the smoke and they began to ride.

"Did he really hang up in my face? Thought Cadence.

This dude has lost his mind.

Cadence began to cry hysterically.

I just told him I was pregnant and he hung up.

She thought about her life. "I am an up and coming lawyer, irresponsible, and unmarried my mother Jezzie is going to kill me when she finds out!"

"How am I supposed to take care of a baby. I'm scared and he hangs up on me!"

Cadence's mind was racing 100 miles per hour.

She had no clue what she should do. She was never really big on making her own decisions. She always needed a little extra help, but who could she talk to.

She couldn't tell Jezzie, and Khalil was ignoring her.

She decided to make a doctor's appointment. She knew that this would be the next best thing to do.

She would call the clinic on 79th and Cottage and request an appointment. It was in the hood, but she could get in and out without telling anyone about the situation.

She wondered if she could really handle a baby right now.

Did she really have the guts to walk through life pregnant, unmarried, and with a father who wouldn't be around or would she get an abortion.

It seemed like a quick fix. Right?

She knew that if she got an abortion she wouldn't have to worry about the aftermath of it all! She wasn't going to keep driving herself crazy.

She picked up the phone and dialed the number to the clinic.

A soft voiced lady answered. "Hello!" "Cottage Clinic. How may I help you?" Cadence quickly hung up.

Do they have caller id? Will they know it is me? Then she stopped in her tracks. Obviously they will know it's you Cadence you have to go INTO the doctor. She thought to herself. I have got to chill. I got myself into this situation and I have got to find a way to make this right.

She redialed the number. "Cottage Clinic" said the soft voiced lady.

Cadence replied "I-I-I wanna make an appointment. I think that I am pregnant."

"What makes you think that you are pregnant?" asked the lady.

"I haven't had my cycle in 2 months."

"Oh. Replied the lady. You can come in today between 9 a.m. and 2 p.m." Cadence thought "Wow. That's quick!"

"Okay Cadence replied, do I need to bring anything?"

"No just bring yourself pregnancy test are free. If you are deciding to have a procedure done you will need an I.D or insurance card and at least $250 depending on your discount."

Thank you replied Cadence and she hung up the phone.

$250 she thought to herself.

That's the price of ending a life!

Cadence decided to go to the clinic first and then think about calling Khalil later.

It was a Saturday morning and after her eventful night of sweating Khalil she was exhausted. Between fear and anger she had nothing left in her.

Cadence hopped in the shower, and found some loose fitting clothing to wear.

She thought about calling her ride or die Tiny, but she knew this was something she had to do alone.

She grabbed the keys and locked the door to her apartment.

Cadence pressed the car alarm and hopped in.

The clinic wasn't far at all from her house and since it was so early it wasn't at all crowded either.

Cadence looked around the clinic and even though she had driven down this street millions of times the funeral home across the street stood out supremely on this day.

She felt death.

She tried to shake the feeling but it was heavy like a fog of thick smoke.

Cadence parked the car in the lot and shuffled quickly into the clinic.

Cadence saw a couple of women sitting in the waiting area.

She walked up to the window that had thick glass with a hole for speaking. She began to speak "I need to get a pregnancy test."

The older gray haired lady looked Cadence over. Then she spoke "Fill this out."

Cadence recognized the voice as the voice that was on the phone when she called. The lady's demeanor over the phone was that of a loving grandma, but in her presence you could sense that she didn't like her line of work.

She looked Cadence over as if to ask with her eyes "Why was she here?" Cadence responded with a blank look in her eyes as to say "I don't even know!"

Cadence looked over the paper.

The half slip of white paper with black ink read as followed. Name: Cadence Edwards. Date of Birth: September 8, 1980. Last cycle date: Unknown. Cadence returned the paper to the window.

The older lady looked it over. She said "Wait here." Cadence stood there slightly irritated because she was at the front of the office and all eyes seemed to shift from the televisions to her.

The lady returned she gave Cadence a plastic cup with an orange screw on top. She also handed her a small key attached to an oversized slab of wood. Cadence took the items and waited for further instructions.

"Go out the door and make a left. Go down the hall all the way to the end the bathroom is on your left. Make sure you push the door hard, it gets stuck, and don't forget to bring back the key. Fill up the cup and bring it back with you."

Cadence nodded her head and proceeded for the door.

She turned left and looked down what seemed to be a mile of a hallway. The walls were a boring oatmeal color and the carpet was a dusty brown. Everything in the place reminded Cadence of death.

She could not believe she had gotten herself into this predicament.

She had become what she perceived to be a statistic.

And to add icing to the cake of horror was the fact that Khalil wanted NOTHING to do with her. She finally after what seemed like an hour reached the bathroom. She pushed the peach colored door and felt the wall for the light. Cadence flicked the light and the bathroom dimly lit up.

She turned to the sink and noticed a metallic sheet metal mirror.

She looked at her distorted image and began to cry.

She didn't REALLY need these results.

She already knew she was pregnant.

She was in this alone and was extremely upset with herself.

Cadence wiped her tears, and turned toward the toilet. She filled the plastic cup to the rim with her urine and screwed on the orange top. She grabbed a wad of tissue and wiped off the specimen cup in an effort to not return it to them soaked with urine.

She placed the precious cup on the sink, and grabbed another wad of tissue to wipe herself. She pulled up her pants and looked in the metallic sheet mirror.

I am way too young to be a mother.

So how am I a mother?

Then she stepped into the sea of denial.

"Maybe I'm tripping," she thought. My cycle never comes on time anyway. I'm sure it will be negative, and can go back to my life."

Cadence grabbed the specimen with a newfound hope and skipped happily down the long oatmeal-colored hall.

When she reached the clinic office she pushed the door. The older lady motioned her into the office, and she put the specimen on the counter where she pointed.

Cadence placed the urine right above the paper she filled out with all her information.

She went into the waiting room and grabbed a magazine to pass the time. She flicked through the pages slowly pretending to read each article, but didn't have the concentration to focus on anything at this moment. She began to think about what she would do for the rest of the day when her thought process was interrupted.

"Edwards" called the older lady.

Cadence got up and went through the office to a back room.

The counselor in the back said "We have your results."

She proceeded.

She handed Cadence back her paper face down.

As Cadence slowly began to turn the paper over the counselor spoke.

"You're pregnant! What are your plans?"

Cadence didn't hear correctly.

She thought the counselor whose visual appearance declined tremendously after she spoke said she was pregnant.

Cadence turned over her information paper and at the bottom there it was in black and white the box checked POSITIVE.

"WHAT?" screamed Cadence in disbelief as if she had never engaged in sexual activity before in her life?

What do you mean pregnant?

The counselor looked at Cadence perplexedly.

"Have you been sexually active? "

She asked sarcastically with an ounce of confusion.

Cadence stared into space for a moment.

Her hearing had temporarily left her.

Everything sounded like a blur.

The counselor spoke a bit louder.

"CADENCE, have you or have you not been sexually active? Now sounding a bit agitated." Cadence snapped back to reality and responded.

"Huh?"

The counselor was beyond her point of patience and allowed the hood in her to slip out.

"GIRL, have you been having sex or what?

Why are you sitting here acting like you're the Virgin Mary and a baby has been placed in your womb."

Cadence was pissed at the counselor, but admitted to herself that she had been tweaking. Cadence responded

"Yeah I've been having sex."

The counselor preceded now code switching back to her professionalism.

"What is your plan?"

Cadence thought for a moment.

She honestly replied "I don't have a plan! I was hoping I wasn't pregnant."

Cadence grabbed her result paper and bag and scurried out the door.

She tried to hold the tears until she got to the Sunfire, but she couldn't deal

. Before she reached the front door the tears flowed like the River Nile. She walked quickly to the car and opened the door and plopped down.

She looked at the paper through tear-filled eyes.

"I'm screwed she screamed!"

Chapter 11

Khalil had been ignoring Cadence for about four days now.

He couldn't lie he was a bit nervous about the pregnancy scare and really wanted to know what was going on, but he had also been dealing with the Dirty Dozen and their crazy drama. Mikey, Cheese, Big Boy, Ralph, and Jabar were running amuck.

Tommy was distant trying to get to the money.

And then there was Reckless.

Reckless was new to the hood, and the name spoke for itself. He was a live wire ready to pop off at any given moment. One day while on the block the Dirty Dozen had heated dice game brewing. Reckless was in the cut taking everybody's bread. Cheese faded Reckless on the dice for the dub. Cheese loss and went to pick up the dub. Reckless was heated. "Why you reaching for my dub bro?" Cheese continued to pick up the money "You don't even need this. I'm trying to fade somebody else with this, and I need......" Before Cheese could finish his sentence Reckless reached back and slapped spit from Cheese's mouth.

Cheese dropped the dub and started charging at Reckless.

Khalil stepped in between the two in an effort to stop the forthcoming World War.

Cheese spoke "How you gonna let this dude slap me? He ain't even from the hood! He ain't got no reason being over here, let alone touching me, or keeping my money."

Khalil thought for a moment.

Reckless wasn't from the hood so Cheese had a bit of validity in his argument, but right was right and wrong is wrong.

Cheese was wrong for trying to take Reckless' money period!

"Cheese you can't be on no Tough Tony mess trying to take somebody money and then when they get on that with you you wanna say they ain't from over here!"

"He's part of the Dirty Dozen right? He stay on the Drive right? He from over here just like everybody else is!"

Cheese was pissed!

He felt like Khalil was supposed to be on his side.

The underlying hate he felt for Khalil was beginning to surface like a pimple about to burst.

It was hard for Cheese to hide how he was starting to feel about Khalil.

This was the beginning of Cheese turning on Khalil and ill intent was about to start showing in more ways than one. Khalil could see the shift in Cheeses' body language and he knew the position he took wasn't sitting with him well, but Khalil couldn't get stuck on feelings he had to go with the righteous move.

Reckless wasn't wrong for wanting his bread, and Cheese was wrong for trying to block bully him.

Cheese looked at the Dirty Dozen and said "I'm out B!"

He hopped in the Impala and pulled off.

He was heated.

He could heat a kettle of water with the steam that was coming from his head. "Every dude over there got me messed up! Who do they think I am? I'm finna stunt on everybody. That's my word, and my word is bond."

Cheese picked up his phone "Tiny I'm out front let's roll."

Tiny replied "Here I come baby!"

Tiny yelled bye to her mother and stepped out the apartment door.

She walked to the passenger side door and got in.

She smiled at Cheese lovingly and he looked and said "What's up?"

She leaned over to kiss Cheese but he was too mad to even kiss her back.

"Cheese what's wrong" said Tiny.

Cheese replied "I just left the block and that weak dude Khalil been hating on me! He just took some random dude side over mine, and I'm through with him! I'm finna stunt on bro no b.s.!"

Tiny didn't say anything.

She took a mental note and kept it moving.

They rode in silence for the remainder of the ride.

Cheese was trying to figure out how to hurt Khalil in more ways than one!

Back on the block Khalil began to politic with Reckless.

"Reckless you can't have emotional responses to everything that someone does. You gotta be a thinker! You got think pass go or you're gonna end up in some really bad situations."

Reckless listened to Khalil, but applying what he was learning was difficult for him.

"All I know is disrespect begets disrespect" said Reckless.

He was mad disrespectful for trying to take my money. I gave him the opportunity to make it right and he kept at what he was on with no regard for me! So why would I have any regard for him?"

Khalil didn't even know how to answer that question.

Reckless was really right!

Forget it bro replied Khalil.

Let's smoke.

He'll get over it.

Khalil was about to go into his pocket and get the smoke and felt a "buzz".

He looked at his phone screen: CADENCE.

Khalil couldn't take it anymore.

He walked down the block a little to separate himself from the crowd.

He answered the phone "Hello".

He listened intently for Cadence's voice on the other line.

"Hello" Cadence replied.

Khalil could hear the sobs and anguish in her voice.

He knew he had messed up and he had no idea how he could fix this.

His heart ached because he knew she was hurt.

"I'm pregnant. I went to the clinic and they gave me a test."

Khalil's heart dropped.

He didn't want to kill his baby, but he didn't want a baby either.

"So what you gonna do?" said Khalil. "I think you should get an abortion we ain't ready for no baby man!"

Cadence was so disappointed!

She didn't really want an abortion, but she didn't want to go at this alone either.

"I guess I'm getting an abortion then" Cadence replied.

"It costs $250 and I don't have it at this moment!"

Khalil listened as he thought about the money he just jagged at the club and the fact that he just went back to the store for the work so he didn't have $250 in cash either.

"Give me a couple of days to put it together Cadence and I'll get it to you! Trust me I got you!" Cadence was angry.

A couple of days she thought.

So I am supposed to let this baby keep growing in me?

She knew a couple of days to Khalil meant at least a week or two.

She couldn't take any chances playing with him.

"Alright" Khalil she replied.

He started to say something else and looked at the phone and noticed that the call had ended.

He wanted to call back, but didn't know the words to say.

He pulled the smoke out his pocket and pushed the phone back in.

Then he walked back to the Dirty Dozen and put the conversation he had with Cadence to the back of his mind.

Chapter 12

Give him a couple of days!

Give him a couple of days!

"I can't let this baby keep growing in me." thought Cadence.

She was sick to her stomach literally and pissed that she had gotten herself into this stupid ass situation.

What she did know is that she couldn't let a baby keep growing in her knowing she was going to have an abortion.

Waiting on Khalil was out of the question!

She only had one option left: JEZZIE!

She knew Jezzie would tear her a new anus, but she had no choice.

How can I break it to Jezzie? She thought about taking her to dinner or sending a text. Cadence was actually terrified of telling her mom face to face no matter how old she was.

I'll just call her and tell her while she's at work.

That way she can work through her anger before she gets off, and I she won't come to my apartment trying to murder me.

Now...when's a good time to call she thought.

Cadence felt the pressure to get things done with the situation.

She felt like the more she waited the more of a "baby" the cells were becoming.

"I'll call now! She said aloud breaking her own silence.

Cadence picked up her phone and dialed Jezzie's number.

The phone began to ring, and Cadence could feel her heart pounding like crazy.

She knew that if her heart wasn't protected by her rib cage it would have ejected from her body and been pumping on the floor. Cadence began to visualize it coming to pass and as soon as her heart was about to hit the pavement her daydream was interrupted with

"Hello." Jezzie spoke softly because she was at the office.

Cadence replied "Hey Mama."

"What's up Cadence?" Jezzie spoke with such gentle care.

Cadence hesitated and slowly said "Ma-Ma-Ma" Jezzie interrupted "Girl, you ain't no baby! What's the problem?"

Cadence took a deep breath and continued "Mama I'm pregnant!"

Jezzie was silent for what had to have been ten minutes.

"You're what?" Cadence repeated herself

"I'm pregnant Mama!"

You could hear Jezzie begin to weep. "So what do you plan on doing?"

Cadence was frightened.

"I don't know Mama. I'm not ready for a baby."

Jezzie continued to weep.

"Cadence I can't help you raise a baby! I wanted more for you then I had for myself! You aren't married, or responsible, and is he even going to help you?

Cadence understood where Jezzie was coming from.

It wasn't going to be just Cadence's baby it would be Jezzie's baby too!

"You should consider getting an abortion Cadence!" said Jezzie.

The next thing Cadence heard was the dial tone!

Cadence sat there with the phone still to her ear hoping for her mother to say more, but she didn't.

Cadence swallowed her fear and morals in one big gulp and called Cottage Clinic.

"Hello Cottage Clinic" said the soft voiced lady.

My name is Cadence Edwards and I want to make an appointment for a procedure she said.

"What kind of procedure are you referring to? Asked the lady.

Cadence walked to the bathroom as her stomach began to turn in knots

She looked in the mirror and replied "I need an abortion!"

The lady on the phone said okay I have Wednesday at noon available. Does that work for you? Cadence rubbed her belly and said "It'll have to!

Khalil had been grinding like crazy!

He knew he needed to get Cadence the $250 she needed to handle the business.

He really didn't want her to get and abortion, however he could not have a baby right now!

$250 was nothing to Khalil; he spent that eating and kicking the bobo-bobo's.

The problem was so much was going on he didn't have the street product he needed to make the money to give to Cadence.

Khalil felt the pressure though.

He knew if Nadine found out about Cadence and the baby that was all she wrote.

Cadence would be having his baby with no questions asked. Nadine d5id NOT believe in abortions, and "I ain't ready for a baby" definitely wasn't going to be the rebuttal to help her change her mind.

Khalil thought about just getting the bread from one of the guys to give to Cadence, and then just hitting them once the work started rolling in, but he really didn't want to put anyone in his business.

He sat quietly in the forest green Concorde thinking of a master plan when his thoughts were interrupted by the vibrating of his phone.

He was a bit taken aback and didn't even want to look at it hoping it wasn't Cadence calling about the money.

He looked down and at the phone and read the screen: Reckless!

He sighed a breath of relief and answered enthusiastically.

"Reckless my boy, what's to it?"

Reckless chuckled his sinister laugh, and got straight to the point.

"What's this I hear about beef between you and Cheese?"

Khalil thought to himself "Beef".

Khalil had forgotten all about the confrontation with Cheese. For him it was water under the bridge, but he was from a different breed. The type who couldn't accept self-correction, and use it for self-growth, plus for Khalil "beef" meant hoodies, black masks, and gun play, and Cheese wasn't ready for that type of smoke.

Just as Khalil was about to reply his line beeped: CHEESE.

He knew the next move, and told Reckless to hold on and let him get the other line right quick.

Khalil clicked over and said "Cheese what's up?"

Cheese replied "nothing".

"I'm just trying to get my halsted out the cut with everybody else's move!"

Khalil thought to himself "Aww. We do have beef!"

Khalil proceeded to reply.

"Well why would you wanna do that bro when this is the way we've been getting money for months now, and it works. Why mess with something that isn't broken? Plus what's this I'm hearing about us having beef?

Cheese took the phone from his ear and looked at it. How could Khalil possibly already know about his ill-feelings towards him. He knew it was in his best interest to sweep it under the rug so he thought carefully about his reply.

"Man I ain't got beef with you bro, you was bogus for that stunt you pulled at the dice game, but it is what it is. I'm just trying to get my money and stay out the way."

Cheese smirked after he finished just knowing that he had thrown Khalil off of his trail.

Khalil chuckled "Alright my dude, my bad for whatever I did to you. I think it's best that we keep the operation working the way it has been. Everybody's getting money so let's keep it that way!"

Cheese agreed. "You're right let's get to it!" he replied although he was fuming on the inside.

Khalil was exhausted with the situation and told Cheese he would hit him back.

He returned to the line with Reckless "What Beef?"

Reckless began his rant!

He started with what the streets had told him.

Khalil tried to pay attention to him, but the noise from his thinking outweighed Reckless' rants.

Khalil thought about how Cheese was his brother, but he knew that things were changing. He could feel the tension in the air.

Khalil decided to make a mental note of it, but to keep it moving he couldn't let Cheese be a distraction for him.

He had one thing on his mind: MONEY!

Money was the motive for Khalil, and the work was on the way.

He knew he was close to financial success and he could almost taste it.

He saw himself in that new Maserati, and like a cloud of smoke it disappeared.

Khalil's phone rang: CADENCE.

Suddenly he was back to reality!

He pressed ignore and thought about how he could get this money quickly.

He began to feel sweat dripping down the nape of his neck. It was getting hot in the Concorde. He had been sitting there talking for what seemed like hours. He got out to stretch, and saw the black on black thang rolling down the block.

Tommy pulled the window down.

"What's to it foolie?"

Khalil replied "Chillin bro, what you on?"

"I'm finna slide to this boat", replied Tommy.

Boat thought Khalil.

Tommy continued "You down?"

. Khalil thought to himself. "Why not go? I ain't doing nothing else, and I could definitely get away from the pressure of the block."

Khalil replied "I'm down! Let me lock the doors of the Green Thing!"

Khalil unknowingly agreed to the beginning of his demise.

Chapter 13

The dimly lit sign outside of Cottage Clinic looked like signage out of a horror movie.

Wednesday arrived more quickly than Cadence anticipated, and she was dreading the walk down the oatmeal colored hallways.

She didn't want to get an abortion, but she wasn't strong enough take care of the baby on her own.

Cadence knew she couldn't handle the judgement or the financial responsibility, but she loved her unborn child.

Khalil was too busy to go to the clinic with her so she called Tiny her trusted compadre. Cadence needed encouragement. So Tiny was her go to!

Tiny reassured Cadence that everything would be okay as they entered the door to the clinic.

Cadence wanted so deeply to believe her, but she knew it wasn't a going to be a quick fix like the emotionally void females had tried to convince her.

Cadence got to the front counter at the clinic and rang the bell to inform the staff that she arrived.

Ding.

Silence erupted for what seemed like an hour.

Then the office clerk very sluggishly approached the glass window.

She slid across the glass and asked "Can I help you?"

Cadence looked back at Tiny to see if she saw the attitude that the clerk had, but her face was stuffed in a fashion magazine. Fashion was Tiny's existence. It was her dream to one day own a boutique, and getting "dressed up" was the highlight of her life.

Cadence turned back to the clear glass and softly whispered "I have an appointment for an abortion."

The office clerk looked Cadence in her face, and slightly tilted her body and loudly said "DOC. YOUR NOON ABORTION IS HERE!!!"

Cadence's face immediately began to burn with anger.

She could have reached through the glass window and slapped spit from the clerk's mouth.

Instead she opted out of the idea she was there for a reason, and a job needed to be done.

Cadence sarcastically said thank you and headed to a seat next to Tiny.

Tiny peeked up from her fashion magazine, and said "Did she have to put you on blast like that G?"

Cadence looked at Tiny dumbfounded and began to speak obscenities, but was interrupted by the office clerk's voice.

"Edwards come to the back!"

Cadence looked at Tiny.

Cadence was sure Tiny could feel her fear, because Tiny said "It will be fine!"

Cadence slowly walked toward the back not knowing what to expect.

Once Cadence reached the back room the fear began to paralyze her. She contemplated getting up and leaving, but the fear of having a child was more prevalent than the clinic.

The Doctor began to speak.

"Hello Cadence."

"According to my records you are here for a D&C procedure. Correct?"

Cadence shook her head in agreement.

The doctor continued.

"Well let me give you a quick rundown. Since you opted against being put to sleep the actual procedure is only about 5 min. You will feel tugging and pulling, and may experience extreme cramps. You will have an hour recovery after the procedure, and we will give you medicine that needs to be taken in its entirety. Do you understand?"

Cadence nodded in agreement.

"Is anyone making you get the procedure?" Cadence shook her head no.

The doctor proceeded.

"Well let's move forward. We will need to do an ultrasound just to see how far along you are. Please lay on this table."

Cadence followed the doctors' orders.

The doctor used a cold gel on her stomach and what looked like a microphone to confirm the pregnancy.

She printed out ultrasound pictures for Cadence's medical file.

Cadence really wanted to see the baby.

She was nervous, scared, and afraid. She slowly began to speak.

"May I have one of those ultrasound pictures?"

The doctor turned around and looked at Cadence coldly.

She replied as if her heart resided in Antarctica

"No. If you wanted pictures of your baby you wouldn't be here!"

The doctor then turned around and walked out the room.

Cadence felt her heart sink to the pit of her stomach.

She wanted to get up and run out of the clinic as swiftly as she possibly could, but what would Jezzie say?

How would Khalil feel, and how would life as she knew it be if she left with the baby still growing inside her?

Cadence went against her better judgment, changed clothes and placed her things in the rows of lockers. She walked down the oatmeal colored hallways to the chop shop.

She could smell and feel the death, but she was already dead inside.

What else could she do?

The bright lights of the boat were enthralling.

The excitement of the boat was like a vacation for Khalil.

Khalil began to light up on the inside.

He left the Dirty Dozen, Cadence, the baby, and any other problems at the dock.

When they left shore Khalil felt like he got away from it all.

Khalil found a home at the Black Jack table.

The excitement of getting 21 and beating the dealer was like a high.

Khalil walked into the boat with $200.

He knew he needed that $200 to get Cadence out the way, but he had to make the other $50 so he thought it wouldn't be a big deal to just use that to play.

Khalil sat at the Black Jack table with Tommy for 6 hours.

The time went so swiftly he didn't even realize he had been there for so long.

He had ate, drank, kicked it, and made some money.

It was cool, Khalil thought.

He didn't have an addictive nature so knew he could go to the boat and be fine.

The boat was an exaggerated gambling high in comparison to shooting dice on the street.

There was more money to be made, and less of a risk of going to jail.

Khalil was a gambler by nature, but this: This was different.

It was an escape!

An excursion!

It was fun!

Anything involving gaining money was interesting to Khalil, because money was the motive.

Khalil hadn't realized that his phone didn't get service on the boat.

When he looked down he was out of range of any cell towers.

He quickly remembered all the money that needed to be made on the block and snapped back to reality.

Tommy was ready to leave too!

He had had enough also, and he knew he also had moves to make.

Khalil left the boat with a little under a stack.

"That was a decent little stain Tommy."

Khalil had more than tripled his money and did it all while chilling, and not being bothered with the pigs.

Khalil and Tommy rode the elevator to the top floor to retrieve the black on black thang and get back to business.

Tommy went to the trunk and grabbed a fifth of Patron and proceeded to open it.

Khalil grabbed the sleeve of plastic cups off the passenger side door and Tommy poured them both a drink.

They turned the music up and hopped on the skyway to shoot back to the block.

They rode in silence not to disturb each other's train of thought, but in an effort to live in the moment.

They both were nodding their heads to the beat, and in their own worlds.

Tommy pulled up to the Green Thing.

Khalil proceeded to get out.

"I'm about to go pick up that work now K! I'll hit you in like an hour or two after I make my run."

Khalil nodded "I'll be around. It's time to get to...Before Khalil could finish his sentence he felt his phone vibrating like crazy.

"I must have just hit a cell tower he thought to himself."

He looked at the screen of his phone:

Mikey: missed call. Big Boy: missed call. Big Boy: missed call. Cadence: missed call. Cadence:missed call. Cadence: missed call. Mikey:missed call. Reckless: missed call. Cadence text: CALL ME NOW!!!!

Before Khalil could begin to dial a number his phone rang: CADENCE.

He thought about ignoring her call, but he knew he couldn't ignore her forever.

Khalil actually loved Cadence even though he had a despicable way of showing it.

Khalil answered the phone. "Hello."

Cadence went off on a tangent.

Khalil couldn't hear a word she was saying.

Cadence was screaming at the top of her lungs. Khalil got stern.

"Cadence chill! I can't hear a word you're saying!"

Cadence took a deep breath. "Khalil I told my mom. I went earlier today and got the abortion. I kept calling you, and you didn't answer. I was alone and didn't know what to do." Cadence began to weep.

Khalil felt her pain

. He knew he was wrong, but he was also angry.

"Cadence WHY WOULD YOU DO THAT?"

"I told you to wait on me to give you the money. Why didn't you trust me?

Cadence started to cry more.

Khalil's heart sank. He wanted to take her pain away, but he didn't know how.

Khalil didn't know what to say.

He couldn't stand to hear Cadence cry either.

Khalil began to speak. "Cadence I can't take this right now. It's gonna be alright though. I promise we will be cool!" "Just wait and see! I promise!"

Khalil half-way believed himself.

He knew he had some love for her, but he didn't know where it would take them.

What he did know was that he didn't want her hurting.

He thought about stopping by her house, but he knew she probably needed some space. Khalil never intended to hurt Cadence, but sometimes things just happened!!

Chapter 14

It was summertime Chi and it was bussin.

All the little booties were outside and Khalil was in his own personal heaven.

Yeah he loved Cadence, but he was addicted to The Life.

He had been in the game now for 7 years strong, and he knew turning around wasn't an option. He loved the cars, clothes, money, and girls. It all was like an intricate puzzle that he knew he had to solve.

The block was the place to be as usual. When you looked down the tree lined block, in the seemingly residential area you thought you were in a small suburbia.

One block away you had the calming essence of the lake, but once you started to see things for what they really were you knew you were far away from suburbia.

This was the EAST SIDE notorious for murder, crime, and drugs.

Khalil sat in the middle of the block on a stomp next to the "White House".

He thought about the East Side and its glory.

He knew that he was living in a history making time for the block and he was proud to be at the forefront, but conspicuously in the background of it all.

The Dirty Dozen spent most of their time serving from the block so there was always a consistent crowd morning, noon, and night.

You could find your normal drug users, prostitutes, playboys, runners, wifey, and randoms coming through at any moment.

Khalil sat there wondering if he had made the right choices in life knowing that he could have done something different, but he was an excellent street pharmacist, and the streets oozed from his bloodline. It was ingrained and he couldn't really see success at much else.

In the midst of daydreaming about his life he felt his vibration coming from his pocket.

Immediately he snapped back into reality remembering he was on the block, and anything was bound to happen there.

He looked down at his phone and saw the call coming from Cadence, as he flipped up the top of the phone to speak Rafiki walked up.

Khalil greeted Rafiki jokingly "What up mi boi!"

Khalil quickly returned to his call "Cadence I'll hit you right back."

Khalil returned his attention to Rafiki.

Rafiki was a certified Haitian. Tall, skinny, and unattractive in nature, but he kept the women around him like crazy.

Rafiki was a get to the money type of stud, and he would get to it by any means necessary. If it meant he had to rob you, swindle you, or short your work he was the man for the job. Primarily because Rafiki had a supreme understanding of the game he knew he was ugly and he had to pay like he weighed so he made sure to cash out every time.

What Rafiki lacked in appearance he had in heart.

He was essentially a good dude that would enter bad situations in his quest to make money.

Khalil knew this about Rafiki, but he kept him close. He knew Rafiki could potentially be trouble, but "Mi Boy" was a fool wit it, and Khalil loved every minute of it!

Rafiki greeted Khalil with a deep Haitian accent (something he used to be silly or extremely serious at times) "What up Bumbaclot."

Khalil gave a hearty laugh! "What up!"

Rafiki got straight to the point.

"I gotta stain K. You wit it?"

Khalil believed Rafiki always had a stain, because money was the motive, but right now wasn't the time it was too much going on to discuss business.

He thought about a way to push Rafiki's comment to the side just for the moment.

"Man Mi Boy we can get to that later, but I see you came to the block prepared with your own flock of booties!"

Rafiki turned towards the Benz he had parked at the end of the block. There were four chicks in the car all smiling and laughing while looking their way.

Rafiki turned back toward Khalil and replied "Yeah I ain't thinking about them though. What's to this convo later."

By this time Rafiki was holding a conversation with himself, because Khalil was up and in motion to the car. He knew that this was the only way to curb the conversation with Rafiki for the moment. There were far too many eyes and ears and if there was one thing he knew about the game was that people talk, and people talk recklessly.

Khalil walked to the car to fake his interest and get Rafiki on another subject knowing it would save him in the long run. Khalil slowly approached the car and dipped his head in confidently speaking

"Hello young ladies!"

Khalil could be extremely respectful and kind or he could be your worst nightmare. He was on his best behavior though.

Rafiki laughed at Khalil!

Rafiki wasn't the respectful type.

He was the cuff her butt and ask questions later type.

Which usually got him one of two responses: He was either cursed out immensely or he got and "I'm wit it" chuckle.

Just as Khalil proceeded to work his magic he saw a familiar car coming down the block. He stepped back from the Benz and repositioned himself in the middle of the block close to the "White House" stomp.

He began to chuckle because he already knew how this would play out.

The Turquoise Sunfire parked a couple of cars up from the stomp and out hopped..................

None other than Cadence and Tiny.

While waiting on Khalil to return her call Cadence received a call from Tiny, and it was just the excuse she needed to ride down on Khalil.

He never got really mad at her for doing it he kinda chuckled, and told her "When you look for stuff you find it!"

Cadence walked toward Khalil as Tiny made her way down the block looking for Cheese.

Khalil gave Cadence the side eye and said "What's up! I told you I would call you back."

Cadence returned his side eye with one of her own. "I know, but Tiny needed a ride over here, and I wanted to see you anyway so I came. You gotta a problem with that?"

Khalil looked her over.

He couldn't stand the way she acted sometimes, but he didn't understand why he loved her either. She was so lame, but that's what he liked.

He replied "Naw Cadence, I ain't gotta problem with that, but what if I wasn't even over here?"

But you are, she replied.

He looked away.

Khalil almost certainly knew what was coming next.

Cadence started.

"So why were you all in that car cheesing from ear to ear?"

I knew it! Khalil thought.

"Man I was just being nice."

Cadence always thought Khalil was looking for other girls.

Khalil just wanted her to understand that some stuff just goes with the game, but she didn't get it at all.

Cadence had a hard time understanding what Khalil went through, and sometimes he just didn't have the time or energy to explain.

Khalil grabbed Cadence by the waist "Let's go to your crib?"

He whispered.

Cadence replied with a fake attitude "What are we driving the Benz you just had your face in?"

"Let's go" Khalil said.

"Are you gonna cook for me?"

Cadence smirked "You always want me to cook for you?"

Khalil led Cadence to the car.

It was way too much going on in the hood today for her to be out here he thought. I'm going to get her put up, and then I'll shoot back to the block later.

Cadence proceeded to leave with Khalil, but then thought about Tiny.

She told Khalil she couldn't leave without her. Khalil yelled down the block to Cheese.

"Aye boy you got Tiny? She good?"

Cheese shook his head, and Tiny smiled.

Cadence knew it was okay to leave then.

As they walked to the Sunfire and proceeded to enter the car Khalil looked at Cadence.

His look demanded her attention, and she looked into his eyes.

He looked at her a bit longer and began to sing "A—l—ways and Forever. Each moment with you." He sang in his best singing voice.

Cadence laughed.

"Get in the car boy" she replied.

He got in the car, and they chuckled together.

As Cadence closed the door and began to put the key in the ignition she turned and looked at Khalil.

He was fumbling with his phone unaware of her looking at him. When he realized the car hadn't started yet he turned to her, and looked stuck. "What's up" he asked with a concerned tone of voice.

"I love you too" replied Cadence.

Khalil smiled.

Chapter 15

Cadence enjoyed spending time with Khalil.

They always had a great time that included endless laughter of some sort.

He was a jokester and she was too.

They pulled up to the two flat building Cadence lived in with and proceeded to go upstairs.

As Cadence was putting the key in the door Khalil started talking "Aye you got some juice?"

Cadence turned around and looked at Khalil like he was crazy.

She didn't understand his obsession with juice primarily because she didn't care for juice, but more importantly she did understand why he would let her drive pass multiple stores on their ride to her house, get out the car, put her key in the door, and then ask about juice.

She replied "I dunno Khalil! You know I don't really drink juice like that!"

Khalil looked crazy now.

"You ain't never got no juice."

There was a deep silence in the hall for what felt like 2 min, and then there was a major abruption of laughter.

Cadence and Khalil laughed so hard Cadence thought she was about to pee on herself.

She hurriedly put the key in the door in an attempt to make it to the bathroom in time.

"Whew" Cadence thought to herself after leaving the bathroom.

Khalil was already in Cadence's room sitting on the bed with the television on.

"What you gonna cook me girl?"

Cadence didn't know what to cook Khalil.

He was the culinary expert he should try cooking.

Every time Cadence cooked Khalil had instructions for her on how to add more seasoning to make the taste just right.

Khalil came from a long line of cooks who specialized in making exquisite hood cuisine.

He didn't know how to cook per say, but he knew what tasted good, and what didn't!

After the laughter and cooking lessons Khalil walked Cadence to her room.

They both knew the inevitable was about to go down.

Cadence always thoroughly enjoyed and hated this part.

Khalil was so busy, and he always had to get to business a short time after they were together.

Cadence knew Khalil loved her, but his actions sometimes made her question it a little.

After Khalil and Cadence spent time being intimate his tune totally changed.

Khalil turned to Cadence and smiled.

He looked her straight in her eyes, kissed her forehead, and said "Hold me!"

Cadence obliged and held Khalil tightly.

She lifted his head from her chest and sweetly asked "What's wrong Khalil?"

He contemplated telling her a lie, but he knew it wouldn't fly with Cadence. There was no hiding things from her. She knew him so well it was almost scary.

Khalil took a deep breath and started "It's so much going on out here in these streets. I'm just trying to get some money and stay out the way! At times that's really hard though."

Khalil knew that was enough to suffice for Cadence.

She knew the game very well, and she knew pillow talking wasn't something they were into.

Khalil would give her a brief synopsis of his problems, and she would comfort him from there.

Cadence replied "Well, do the best you can to stay out of trouble!"

Khalil chuckled "I'm trying man! I'm trying"

Cadence began to say something else, but noticed that Khalil had dozed off to sleep.

Instead of interrupting him she decided to let him sleep. Khalil barely slept at all. He was like a machine running on a 24 hour clock. He seemed to find solace being in Cadences' presence so he snuck in as much "deep" sleep as he possibly could. Cadence closed her eyes and lived in the moment. She took a deep breath, and before she knew she was out like a light.

Two hours later Khalil popped up instantaneously nearly giving Cadence a heart attack.

He sleepily looked around and asked "What time is it".

Cadence replied it's 4:30.

Khalil wiped his eyes and thought "Man it's time to get out here."

"Cadence I gotta go!"

Cadence looked sad, but knew that Khalil had things to do.

She was grateful for the time the spent together and gave him a kiss and hug.

Khalil reached in his coat pocket and pulled out his phone.

He looked at the screen and shook his head. 16 missed calls! Khalil skimmed through the call log to see what he had missed.

Khalil called Mikey.

Mikey was his go to man for the drop off, and pick up! He knew when Mikey said he was on his way. He was on his way. Khalil called Mikey. No answer. Khalil pressed send again, and called Mikey again. No answer. Khalil really didn't want to call anyone else, but was left with no choice.

He looked through his call log, and settled with calling Cheese.

He pressed send and listened to the phone ringing.

After 3 rings he heard loud music and a chuckle coming through the line.

"K what's to it" Cheese answered.

"Aye, I need a ride. I'm at Cadence crib. Who you wit?"

Cheese replied "It's me Ralph, and LB."

LB was Khalil's cousin Ali who got his nickname from his older brother.

LB and Khalil were around the same age so they were thick as thieves.

Khalil replied "Aight come get me, and don't bullcrap Cheese I got moves to make."

Cheese laughed uncomfortably and replied "I'm coming right now dude!"

Khalil began to gather his things and get himself mentally prepared for getting back in the streets.

Cadence was his home, the place where he could relax, and be totally secure.

Khalil was still getting himself together and when he felt his leg vibrating. He took out his phone and looked at the screen: CHEESE.

He answered "I'm downstairs lame!"

Khalil chuckled "I got your lame! Quit playing with me dude."

Khalil looked at Cadence softly.

He took his hands and grabbed her around her waist and pulled her close.

He kissed her forehead, and lifted her face up by gently grabbing her chin. He looked into her eyes and said "Cadence I love you!"

He kissed her lips sweetly, and Cadence held him tight!

After that Cadence didn't want him to leave! She was putty in his hands! She tried to get him to stay, but Khalil replied "Cheese is downstairs! I'll be back baby!"

Cadence kissed Khalil gently, and opened the front door.

Khalil walked out, and turned around and smiled at her!

Cadence felt the love exuding off of Khalil.

She ran to him and kissed him again.

He smiled "Gone now girl! I gotta go!"

Cadence laughed and ran back up the stairs, and locked the door.

It was money time and Khalil had to get to it!

He had spent most of the day with Cadence.

He didn't mind, but he had to catch up with his hustle.

He realized he really loved Cadence.

His mind started to drift to her, but he shook his head and got himself together.

Khalil had an amazing way of compartmentalizing things.

He left the streets in the streets!

He left home at home, and he made it his duty to keep it that way.

Life taught him that having your head in the clouds in the streets meant death!

Khalil got focused.

Ralph opened the car door and smiled a sinister smile.

Khalil laughed! "What's to it bro?"

Nothing! Ralph replied I'm just living.

Khalil closed the car door and heard a loud eruption as if an active volcano was presently erupting.

Cheese gave a half-baked smile and said "I'm too hungry." Let's stop at the gas station on 83rd. I wanna get some snacks or something."

Khalil and Ralph agreed.

They were always down for Super Donut and an ice cold Tahitian Treat.

On the way to the gas station Cheese called Italian Fiesta.

He ordered a large Beef and Cheese, well done, with extra tomato sauce and oregano.

He figured he could take 71st straight to the east side and pick up the pizza on the way.

The snacks from the gas station would hold them off until they got to the pizza and back to the block.

Cheese turned the wheel to the Forest Green Concorde into the Citgo.

Ralph, Cheese, LB, and Khalil all got silent.

Inside the gas station was a sight to see!

It was like a Christmas gift wrapped just for them. Khalil looked at them and gave the green light.

"It's a go!"

Chapter 16

Cadence was on cloud nine!

Khalil was her "everything".

She couldn't believe they had spent the whole day together. It was like a dream come true. If she didn't know anything else she knew that Khalil loved her tremendously.

Cadence was losing focus though, and she felt it!

Her entire life was surrounded around Khalil and what he had going on. No matter what she was in the middle of, she would drop it like a bad habit if Khalil called.

He was like a drug she was totally addicted to.

Cadence was lacking at work, separating herself from her friends, isolating herself from her mother, and not handling her business.

Khalil never asked Cadence to do these things, but she was gone in the head for real.

Cadence needed Khalil.

He was the centerpiece of her little world, and nothing would change that!

She knew she had to get a hold of herself, but she didn't know how.

It was like she was too far gone in this thing with Khalil. She had slowly became a part of his world. Cadence went from the lamest girl on the block with zero street smarts to enjoying the street life.

She was all in with Khalil and she was willing to prove herself to him to help him understand.

Cadence's thoughts of Khalil were interrupted with a loud pounding at the door.

"BOOM BOOM BOOM." she was scared.

She didn't have any contraband in her house at the present time, but nonetheless she knew that it was the police.

Cadence slowly walked to the door.

She whispered softly "Yeeeaaaaah, who is it?"

Tiny chuckled to herself.

She knew Cadence was extremely scared.

Tiny made her voice as deep as possible.

"POLICE OPEN UP."

Cadence thought she was about to pee on herself.

She was scared to death.

She thought she wanted a part of the street life, but the police was one thing she wasn't about to play with.

In that split second she thought to herself "Would you trick on him or go to jail?"

Cadence was too real for TV so tricking wasn't an option, but she ain't want to go to jail either.

She shook her head and erased the thought from her mind. "Let the cards fall where they may."

She thought to herself.

She opened the door and saw Tiny standing there. GIRL!!!!

Cadence thought about slapping Tiny, but that was her girl.

"You play too much!"

"You had me contemplating my life behind that door."

Tiny turned bright red like a reddish laughing hysterically.

She slapped her knee and bent over as if she was watching Dave Chappelle in the Rick James skit.

Cadence was beginning to become infuriated.

"It ain't that funny Tiny."

"I was really thinking about my life behind that door."

Tiny slowly got herself together. She slowed her chuckle down, and tried to gain her composure.

"What were you contemplating?" she asked seriously.

Cadence looked up with a stone serious face.

"I was contemplating if I would trick or go to jail if it were the police at the door?"

Tiny looked at Cadence and seriously asked

"What was the contemplation for?"

Cadence thought in her head.

"What does she mean? That's my man! I ain't never bout to trick on my man!"

Tiny turned into Ms. Cleo and began to read Cadence's thoughts.

"BITCH!!!!!" Tiny yelled while slapping Cadence on the shoulder with a bit of force.

"I KNOW YOU AIN"T GOING TO JAIL FOR NO NIGGA!" "Girl, I would snitch so fast they would wonder if I ever knew dude. I ain't going to jail for nobody! So he can be out here with another girl while I'm in there doing time! Please! My loyalty lies with TINY!!! That's it and that's all! If it ain't good for Tiny I ain't doing it! That's it and that's all!!!"

"That's why I came over here anyway. You need an intervention in real life. Khalil got you gone in the head, and he ain't even thinking about you!" "He is doing him on a regular basis and you're stopping your life trying to be something for him he doesn't even want!" Listen, Cadence there are SO MANY dudes out here. They will give you time, attention, money, heck even the clothes off their backs if they dumb enough. You're wasting your time!"

Cadence wasn't trying to hear Tiny!

She knew Khalil loved her.

Tiny began being Ms. Cleo again said

"You ain't listening! I'll prove it to you." "Call him!" "I bet my life on it he don't even answer your call!"

Cadence looked Tiny in the eyes and politely said "What would you like on your Tombstone?"

Tiny looked at Cadence just as strongly and replied "Nothing cause he ain't finna answer you! He's done with you for the day!"

Cadence reached for her phone, and shifted through her call log.

She got to Khalil's name and pressed send. "Ring, Ring, Ring, Ring, ... You've reached a voicemail box that has not yet been set up."

Cadence ended the call expeditiously and tried to save face!

"He's probably on the block he always answers the second time around. "Tiny gave a forward nod as to give the okay for Cadence to try again. Cadence looked at her phone, and thought to herself "this dude better pick up!" "Ring, Ring, ...You've reached a voicemail box that has not yet been set up."

Cadence had the crap face, and couldn't hide it!

She felt so stupid.

Not to mention the second time around Khalil had promptly sent her to voicemail.

He had spent the whole day with her.

Why would he not answer?

Maybe Tiny was right Cadence thought.

Tiny felt like laying it on Cadence thick. She knew guys like Khalil! She knew their M.O and the games they played all day long. She knew it was against the code to trust these dudes, but Cadence was different and she had fallen for Khalil hard. Tiny knew she had to intervene before Cadence lost herself in Khalil.

Tiny knew just the trick.

"What better way to get over a dude, then to get with another one!"

Tiny had a twisted mentality.

She had older brothers who taught her the game at a very young age. So she operated with "nigga tendencies" by default.

Tiny looked to Cadence and softly said "Sorry friend."

Cadence tried to hold back the tears.

She could begin to feel the lump rising in her throat and she tried to pull it back, but she couldn't. Her eyes began to run like Buckingham Fountain, and it was nothing she could do about it.

"I just don't get it" Cadence exclaimed!

I thought we were on a good page!

I thought everything was going well, but this!

This is crazy to me!

A thought crossed Tiny's mind.

"Maybe he's busy! I mean he is in the streets!" Tiny kept the thought to herself.

She felt it was better for Cadence to bask in her sadness. Whether Khalil was busy or not he was not good for Cadence and Tiny just wanted the best for her friend. Nothing more and Nothing less.

"I think we should go out Cadence."

Tiny said with a sinister look, because going out with Tiny meant dudes were involved in some way, shape, form, or fashion.

Cadence continued to cry.

She was still trying to process it all, but she obliged.

Fully aware of what she was consenting to agreeing to going out with Tiny Cadence spoke in a wavering manner

"I guess I can go out!"

9339!

Who would have thunk it!

At the gas station at the same time as the Dirty Dozen.

Khalil had already given the green light!

It was a go on sight for the crew!

They had been speaking in an ill manner about the Dirty Dozen, and it was enough for all of the members, not just Khalil.

9339 had been ducking and dodging the Dirty Dozen for months now, and it seemed as if they were handed to Khalil on a Christmas platter with a wrapped bow.

LB hopped out the car first on straight dummy!

"Ralph and Khalil followed closely."

Cheese was late to the confrontation as usual. He pretended as if he was parking the car straight, and fidgeted with the cigarette lighter as things began to play out.

Khalil instantly walked up to the biggest member of 9339 and muffed his head so hard it looked as if his neck would snap and his head would separate from his body all together.

The big boy was perplexed he began to speak. "I ju-."

Before he could get the rest of the words out of his mouth Ralph landed a hard right into his cheek. It was followed by a quick left and everything else was a go!

Khalil who was the hood-proclaimed knock-out king found pleasure in the one-hitter quitter.

His goal was to hit you one time and on to the next person to knock out.

Fortunately for 9339 they had numbers in their favor.

Unfortunately, for them they were suburban nerds from the city.

They didn't know the first thing about this hood fight their loose lips had gotten them into, and they were about to sink quickly.

The rest was a blur!

Bodies flew, blood gushed, and Cheese watched it all!

He threw a couple of kicks here and there, and then it got real.

LB was sick of the fighting and went to the car for his trusty sidekick.

He returned to the rumble.

The next thing you heard was the gun cock followed by "Everybody get down!"

Khalil swiftly turned his head to the direction of the voice.

He realized it was LB and knew that things had just gotten superbly real.

There was no turning back now.

Khalil knew what was next, and although he felt like this was a step too far he couldn't turn around "Loyalty over everything" was the motto he lived by so it was a green light.

All of the members of 9339 began to lie on the ground reluctantly.

They had no idea that they would be getting robbed because of some small click shit.

They were not ready at all for what their mouths got them into.

They laid on the ground shaking scared out of their mind as their pockets were ransacked by LB, Ralph, and Khalil.

They took everything as Cheese watched from a short distance.

After laying 9339 down Cheese jumped in the driver's seat of the car and the crew piled in!

Laughs erupted from the car as they discussed how "shook" those dudes were.

They drove down 71st to go back east smoking and drinking and having the time of their life.

They decided as a crew that they weren't going to get rid of the items from the little spat.

They kept them as hood trophies of their conquests.

Cheese, LB, Ralph, and Khalil had no clue what awaited them once they reached the hood, but they would soon find out.....

Chapter 17

And so it was!

Cadence and Tiny were on their way out in these streets.

Cadence looked for something to wear.

She wasn't really ready to go out, but she had to do something.

She wasn't about to get played!

She shuffled through her attire for some club worthy clothing.

She located a navy blue mini skirt, with gray stockings, and a navy blue and gray sheer top.

Cadence added some navy blue heels to complete the attire.

She was on point and ready to roll.

Tiny pulled up out front of Cadence's house and honked twice.

Cadence did a once over in the mirror making sure she looked immaculate.

Tiny honked the horn rapidly for a succession of what felt like 5 minutes.

In the midst of the honking Cadences' phone began vibrating.

"Hey Mama what's up?"

Jezzie began to speak. "I'm just checking on you, what's going on.?"

Cadence began to reply, but was interrupted by Jezzie.

"What is that noise in your background?"

Cadence replied.

"It's Tiny outside honking the horn. I'm about to go out and apparently I'm taking too long!"

Jezzie took a small breath and replied "Ain't no real friend gonna honk the horn for you they are coming upstairs. You need to check your friends!"

Cadence gave Jezzie a quick stare through the phone and immediately remembered she had to remain respectful to her mother.

" I'll call you later mama" Cadence said as she ran swiftly out the door.

Cadence quickly thought about if Tiny was really her friend or not, but she let it go on and jumped in the car.

Tiny smiled and said GIRRRRRLLLLL I just knew you were coming outside looking like a catholic priest, but you killed it! I feel like a proud mama!

We are going to Frost Bar tonight! It's about to be poppin.

Cadence looked at her phone Khalil hadn't called once.

She started to call, but knew it was a waste of time.

She decided to enjoy herself as much as possible since Khalil made sure he always enjoyed himself.

Tiny looked at Cadence "Stop thinking about dude! We are about to have fun tonight! We are about to get Mya and get to it!"

Cadence thought to herself "Tiny and Mya! Uh Oh double trouble!"

She loved them but knew it was going to be a mess going out with them.

When she went out with them in the past it was always lots of liquor, lots of guys, and lots of fun!

Cadence just wasn't the going out type so the club scene literally sucked the life out of her.

She loved to dance "by herself" and loved the music! That was the good part!

Cadence would drink, but never too much because she didn't like the way liquor tasted and she hated staying out late.

She went to bed at 8:30 every night!

So when she stayed up late for the club it took everything in her not to fall asleep.

Tiny looked over to Cadence and said" I gotta plan."

Look in my bag.

Cadence shuffled through her bag looking for what seemed to be an eternity.

She finally asked "What is it that I'm looking for?"

Tiny looked at her in a perplexed manner and replied "The drink!"

Cadence let out a sigh because she had passed the drink multiple times just knowing that this wasn't what she was looking for.

She wasn't ready to start drinking before the club, and barely at all for that matter.

She thought to herself momentarily, "What the heck?"

I might as well!

She looked on the side of Tiny's car door, and her trusty friend didn't fail her at all.

A five pack of plastic cups straight from the liquor store awaited her.

Cadence began to fumble some more through Tiny's purse and around the car.

It was as if Tiny had read her mind (which she often did), Tiny said "It's on the back seat. Pineapple! Your favorite right?"

It was a necessity for Cadence to have a chaser liquor was way too nasty to her to drink it straight.

As Cadence prepared her drink she prepared two more minus the chaser for Tiny and Mya as they were approaching Mya's house within the minute.

The crew was back and fun was the game!

Cadence wondered if she could even hang anymore.

She was definitely about to find out.

Mya jumped in the car excited to be out the house.

She often got overwhelmed with her mother and grandmother breathing down her back. She was an only child and they loved to make sure she was okay.

When she got in the car she took a long deep breath.

"Mannnnnn they suck the life outta me sometimes!

She smiled her sweetest smile as she often did, and reached forward because she knew a drink was waiting for her.

Cadence turned to Mya and asked "What's to it?"

Mya chuckled and replied "To what do we owe the pleasure of your acquaintance?"

Cadence laughed hysterically and responded "Don't do me? I go out! I go out all the time!"

She could feel the uneasiness of the lie she had just told and continued "I just needed a breather that's all!"

Mya shoved Tiny on the shoulder while she was driving and Tiny spilled the beans like Mya inserted a quarter in the oversized gumball machine.

"She was sick of Khalil. You know he plays her like a fiddle and she sits there and listens to the song he plays faithfully as if he were a real life musician."

Cadence began to turn red with fury.

Maybe it was the liquor, maybe it was the sting of the truth, or maybe she felt like she was always being put on Front Street for Khalil and his crap. She knew one thing she talked too much, and she needed to learn to keep her mouth closed, and her business to herself or it would come to haunt her later.

They circled the block of the Frost Bar and found a place to park.

Of course they had to walk a block and Cadence was quickly reminded about why she didn't like clubs.

As they approached the line luckily for them there wasn't a very long wait.

The short, overly buff, Napoleon complex bouncer yelled "Have your I.D's out. It's Pro Baseball Night!"

Cadence turned to Tiny and she grinned a grimace grin!

When they reached the front of the line they checked their Id's and they proceeded to the inside door where a young girl quickly said $20.

Cadence reached in her bag and paid abruptly to get out of the way.

The girls reunited on the inside and were shocked to see how crowded the club really was.

From the looks of outside it was a desert, but on the inside it was overflowing like the river Nile.

They walked to the bar as it was customary to at least buy your own first drink.

Cadence, Tiny, and Mya all ordered a shot of Patron.

Cadence took the first shot quickly she knew you couldn't sip Patron you had to drink it and drink it quick!

It burned as it went down but she took a deep breath and began to tune out to the music.

The lights in the club were vibrant and bright and she felt like she was in her own personal show.

Cadence looked to her left and Tiny was talking to some semi-tall attractive guy.

She leaned close and said this is Smith and he plays baseball.

Smith looked at Cadence and smiled.

Cadence leaned closer to Smith and said Hello.

Tiny repeated the same with Mya.

Smith asked Tiny what we were drinking, and that's where the party began.

Since money wasn't an issue for Smith he kept the drinks coming. He had one intention and that was to get them drunk and hopefully get to home base.

After round seven Cadence couldn't take anymore!

She had tapped out and that was enough.

She couldn't even feel her face, and then reality started to hit hard.

She hadn't heard from Khalil since he left her house earlier that day.

Had he lost his mind? What was going on? It wasn't like him not to call all day long!

Cadence continued to try to have fun, but she really was ready to go.

Tiny and Mya were not!

They looked at their friend and knew the drill!

She was done and ready, but they weren't.

They continued rounds 8, 9, and 10.

The club was about to close and they decided to let Cadence out of her misery.

She was ready to go and they knew it!

Smith wanted to go to another club and Tiny and Mya were down.

Tiny walked to Cadence "There's another bar down here that we can go to."

Before she could finish her sentence Cadence said just take me home.

Mya looked at Cadence seriously and said "You are such a Debbie Downer!"

Cadence blew her off as she checked her phone still in disbelief that Khalil hadn't called her, and filled with pride because she wasn't calling him either.

The ride home was complete silence!

She could feel the tension from her girls and she knew they were ready to get away from her just as much as she was ready to get away from them.

They pulled up to her house and she got out and dryly said "Aight yall!"

Tiny and Mya both replied with the same level of dryness "Yep!"

Cadence knew she would be the topic of discussion as soon as the car pulled off!

Cadence walked to the door with her phone and key in hand.

She put the key into the lock and twisted, and simultaneously her phone rang.

A foreign number popped up on her caller id.

It was 2:30 in the morning.

She thought to herself "Who would be calling me this late from a number I don't know?"

Cadence decided to answer.

"Hello!"

There was a pause on the other line, and then she heard the unthinkable.

"You have a collect call, would you like to accept the charges?"

The ride back East was uneasy for Khalil.

LB, Ralph, and Cheese were in their glory.

They found the act that they just partook in to be rather appealing, but they weren't thinkers.

They continuously lived in the moment.

This was a practice that didn't fare too well in the streets.

You needed the ability to think, pass go, and have a full understanding that every action had a consequence, and Khalil was fully aware of this fact.

If Kaleb did nothing else in life he trained his son to be observant of people.

He made sure to teach him to study people, their body language, and their responses.

Khalil had developed into a human lie detector test.

He would watch your language and body for clues of truth or lie.

He almost knew what a person would do next, because he knew people.

As he sat in the back of the car in his own cloud of smoke he replayed the events that had just taken place back over in his mind.

He had zoned so far out it was as if he were in the car alone, although LB, Cheese, and Ralph laughed loudly, played the music on max, and continued to smoke and drink.

Khalil went into reflection mode as he often did!

He thought to himself "Why would LB grab that gun?"

"We did not need to lay those types of dudes down! They were already scared, but that invoked a fear in them that isn't good. Scared people do one of two things: KILL or TRICK!!!"

Khalil took a moment from his own thoughts and began to speak.

"Aye! Cut that down."

Cheese cut down the music since he was the driver.

LB turned around to the back seat, and Ralph looked to his right attentively.

" LB why did you get that burner?"

Everybody looked in disdain.

They couldn't believe Khalil was asking such a question.

LB responded "What do you mean?"

Khalil could tell the uneasiness in his voice.

He knew he had thought what he did was right, and the idea that he was wrong began to shake LB a little. LB shifted his body posture in an attempt to boss up a little.

Khalil repeated his question.

"Why would you get that burner? What was the motive? What point were you trying to prove? Why my dude? I just want to know why?"

Khalil already knew why.

LB was definitely trying to prove a point!

He wanted to make a name for himself.

He was sick of living in the shadows of everyone else, and deep down inside he was really scary, but he had a name to uphold and the pride he attached with that would make him do anything.

Even if it didn't make sense!

Khalil waited patiently for LB to lie.

LB took a moment.

He thought to himself "Khalil thinks he knows everything he always has some mess to say! I snapped today, and laid them fools down the way they should be! He's just mad he didn't have the guts to do it."

LB decided that he wouldn't respond with that answer so he simply shrugged his shoulders and replied

"They got what they deserved!"

Khalil was getting annoyed with LB and his crap.

"Bro." Khalil began.

"Those are some of the lamest dudes in existence. They don't even rock on the same levels we rock on. There was absolutely no reason to lay them down. The good ole fashion ass kicking they just got would have been sufficient. Those types of dudes get scared and do one of two things KILL or TRICK!"

"I rocked with you, because loyalty over everything and I ain't wanna embarrass you out there, but that was some of the dumbest shit I've seen from you."

Cheese was pulling the car over the tracks on Exchange as they were getting closer to the block.

Khalil was so ready to get away from these dudes.

He knew their mental capacity couldn't yet grasp what was playing out, but HE knew it wasn't gonna be good.

In an attempt to save face LB puffed up and turned around and yelled "What are you scared or something?"

Khalil's first response was to punch LB in the face, but he withheld the urge and simply replied "You just needed something to say huh?"

LB got even more pissed, because Khalil didn't engage him.

So he reiterated his question into a statement.

"You MUST be scared!!!"

Khalil knew fighting LB was a fixed fight.

LB couldn't handle Khalil's hands and he knew it.

If he fought him he would reinforce the same stupid cycle that LB just pulled at the gas station.

Khalil leaned over and looked LB in the eyes and sternly said if I'm scared then you must live mortified. LB was fuming.

He felt like Khalil had been getting the best of him for years.

Cheese smiled internally and prayed on Khalil's downfall daily as he wanted to be the man and the only thing in his way was Khalil.

He played his role to the fullest extent though never blowing his own cover, but he secretly hated Khalil and wanted nothing more than for him to be out of the way.

Ralph on the other hand pushed his back to the seat and replayed the thoughts in his mind.

He was always a listener and a thinker.

He just had the habit of getting caught in the moment and not being able to think his way through, but when he reflected on the situation he knew they had messed up.

Khalil thought to himself "This has got to be the longest car ride over East."

His thoughts were interrupted by Ralph's words.

"Aye y'all he's right. Those dudes ain't pose no type of threat to us. Period!! What they made us lose some little booties? That's it! Girls? They ain't threaten our life or our money! It wasn't that serious! Scared people do scary stuff!!"

LB laughed hysterically and in a mocking voice repeated "You know he's right! Scared people do scary stuff! You are the biggest jock smuggler I know!

Ralph lunged to punch LB in the face. He didn't possess the same restraint that Khalil did, but mid lunge Khalil grabbed him and said "He ain't worth it!"

Ralph leaned back and ordered Cheese to park so they could get out!

As soon as Cheese put the car into reverse he turned and told the guys "Ya'll trippin everything will be fine!"

He sharply turned the wheel to the right and moved the car back some, and as he proceeded to turn left there were swarms of police cars coming his way.

He swiftly put the car into drive so he could get out of their way so they could go about their business and they could theirs, but the four police cars stopped right by his car.

Khalil dropped his head in anguish!

"I told y'all goofies they would KILL or TRICK, and they ain't no killers!

"GET OUT OF THE CAR!!!! PLACE YOUR HANDS IN THE AIR!!"

Khalil, Cheese, Ralph, and LB slowly reached for the handles of the car doors all with one hand in the air.

They made it their business to be sure that they showed their other hand to avoid any unwarranted shots being fired at them.

They knew the police had a way of justifying murdering people and they definitely didn't want to become a part of that ever growing statistic.

They all slowly made their way out of the car.

" PUT YOUR HANDS ON THE HOOD" the police stated with guns drawn.

"YOU TWO IN THE FRONT TURN AROUND."

Cheese turned slowly, but started to speak "Officer why are we being arrested? I didn't I mean--- We didn't do anything.

If looks could kill Khalil would have murdered Cheese on the spot!

What did he mean I didn't!

The heart speaks the truth you just gotta listen. Khalil thought.

He knew right then that Cheese would be shaky throughout this whole dilemma he showed this hand and Khalil peeped the Joker!

"YOU KNOW WHAT YOU DID, AND YOU KNOW WHAT THIS IS!!! SAVE YOUR WORDS FOR YOUR LAWYER!! SHUT YOUR MOUTH AND PUT YOUR HANDS ON THE HOOD NOW!!!"

Cheese turned around and put his hands on the hood.

LB and Ralph were in their own worlds trying to figure out what was going, but when he looked at Khalil across the hood of his car he felt him peering into his soul.

He knew he had messed up, but he didn't think anyone was going to catch it, but Khalil did!

Cheese diverted his eyes away from Khalil.

He couldn't stand the stare.

He put his head down on the hood and closed his eyes.

When everyone had their hands on the hood the police officers slowly walked over and handcuffed their new found suspects.

The law says innocent until proven guilty, however the way that it actually worked was that you were guilty until proven innocent.

Khalil knew that and he knew that this wasn't going to be a little trip to the station.

He figured he would be on an extended stay!

The four cars each transported one of the guys to the station.

The police wanted them separated to ensure that stories weren't being corroborated in the back of the squad cars.

Khalil was actually relieved that he wasn't in the car with any of them, because he knew he would have had an additional charge to deal with, because of the level of stupidity this act was and how he knew it was going to cost him some of his life.

They arrived at the station rather quickly seeing how it was right up the street. 71st had to have the worst police station in the city!

Although it looked newly remodeled on the outside the inside looked like the grim reaper resided there.

The white tiles were yellow stained from all of the detainees' urine.

The place reeked of feces, urine, and homelessness.

The holding cells were freezing like a below zero Chicago winter night.

Not only were the facilities ridiculously disgusting they had to have taken all of the incompetent officers and decided to make this the training center for them. They were rude, lacked information, and had no interest in the prosperity of the public! They were basically there for a check and you could feel that as soon as you walked into the building.

Khalil had his run in with this particular station on many occasions. His wrap sheet was as long as Santa's imaginary "good list".

He hoped that they would have taken him to 51st, but because they had gotten all the way back over East this was his assigned station.

"What luck!" Khalil thought.

They threw all four boys into separate holding cells and left them to their thoughts.

Khalil knew this wasn't going to be a good turnout.

He began to hope for the best possible results out of a bad situation.

He thought "Did those dudes get up off the ground and instantly call the police? We didn't even go anywhere and how did they know where to come? Something ain't right!"

"But if they called the police and made the complaint they hold the cards in their hands so I need to find a way to get to them to have them change their minds or something! Something has gotta give."

Khalil's thoughts were way ahead of his situation, but he was a thinker so he was trying to make a game plan in response to the situation at hand.

Khalil, LB, Cheese, and Ralph were in holding cells for what seemed to be hours.

Khalil heard the clink of the bars and a medium height, round-shaped woman with manly features appeared.

She spoke deeply "GRUB", and dropped a brown paper bag into the holding cell.

Khalil knew the contents of that bag spelled disaster, but he decided to look anyway.

He pulled open the bag and found a "choke".

He looked in disgust!

A bologna sandwich on white bread was a questionable meal at home, but in jail it was the worst. The white bread was thick enough to float on water for hours with no end in sight, and one slice of bologna was as if they took your average grocery store pack of meat and melted them all together.

This wasn't Khalil's first jail rodeo.

He knew exactly how this show went.

He took the sandwich out of the saran wrap.

He began to dissect.

Bread.

Bologna.

Mustard.

His last jail stay was years ago he thought they would have upgraded to at least a slice of cheese or a spread of Miracle Whip, but he knew he couldn't be so lucky.

True to his spirit he made the best out of a bad situation.

Khalil took one slice of bread and did some edge control. He meticulously removed the edges. He proceeded with the same procedure with slice number two. He then took the bologna and made a line of symmetry down the middle. He created a new sandwich with the edible parts of the bread and the piece of bologna that vaguely resembles what people would buy in the store.

He ate because he had to.

He knew that by morning he would be on the County bus on his way to 26th street for his new place of residence The Cook County Department of Corrections.

Khalil began to think about the tan jumpsuits with IDOC plastered on the back.

He couldn't believe that he let these dudes get him into this jam.

It was all bad and he knew it.

Just then he had forgotten he hadn't made a call ALL day.

They guards had failed to give him his one call, and he knew it had to be late now.

GUARD!

GUARD!

Khalil shouted.

He knew he had to play to their emotions to get what he wanted.

"Excuse me Guard, I wasn't able to make my call. Can I do that?"

The guard who was highly pissed that another officer with higher seniority than hers wanted to be moved off the night shift bumped her from her day shift position. She had a permanent attitude. Although she was still fuming at her shift change from weeks ago she couldn't deny Khalil's request especially when he asked so nicely.

"You know it's almost 3 in the morning! Do you have someone who will answer you this late?"

Khalil smiled to himself.

"Yeah I got someone."

The guard removed Khalil from the cell. Khalil proceeded to the phone and dialed the number.

Ring...........Ring.........Ring.........Hello. "Cadence. It's all bad man. I'm on my way to the County and it's gonna be a long ride. I can feel it." "I need you to tell my Momma and look up when I have visiting days and come see me so we can talk." "Hello Cadence. Are you there?"

You have a collect call would you like to accept the charges?

Cadence looked perplexed.

She knew it was Khalil but why would he be in jail.

So this is why he hadn't called her all day.

She felt so stupid about listening to Tiny and going out.

She had fun, but she only wanted to go because she was mad at Khalil.

Cadence shook her head to clear her thoughts and got focused.

"Yes. I accept."

"Hello. Cadence."

Yeah Khalil! What's up?

"It's all bad man." replied Khalil.

I'm on my way to the County and it's gonna be a long ride. I can feel it."

Cadence had a dumb blonde moment thinking to herself the ride from 71st to 26th isn't that far she thought, but then she quickly caught on!

He was going to be in jail for a long time.

Khalil continued.

"I need you to call my momma and tell her and look up when I have visiting days and come see me so we can talk."

Cadence was so angry.

She and Khalil were just beginning to be close and now he was on his way to jail.

Cadence knew nothing about jail and what came along with doing a bid with a man, but she figured she was surely about to be schooled!

"Khalil I don't know what happened, but I love you and I'm going to be here for you."

Time's up Sir! You have to end your call. Khalil took a deep breath.

"I love you Cadence handle the business for me. I gotta go!"

Cadence kept the phone to her ear as if it would extend the time she had with Khalil.

Instead she quickly got the buzzing of the dial tone in her ear.

Cadence peeled the phone from her ear and began to cry hysterically.

Khalil wasn't the type to exaggerate so she knew this was going to be something very deep.

Cadence contemplated whether or not to call Ms. Nadine's house at 3:00 in the morning. Cadence was big on respect especially for Khalil's mother. She decided that this was a very big deal and since Khalil wasn't just going to "get out" she had to inform his mother.

Cadence dialed Ms. Nadine's number with shaky fingers.

After the third ring she opted to hang up but she heard a groggy

"Hello."

Cadence paused out of fear.

She rarely ever spoke to Nadine.

She was very strict about Khalil staying away from women.

Cadence thought how this was the worst possible first time to ever have a conversation with his mother.

"Hello."

Hello Mrs. Nadine.

This is Cadence.

I'm calling because Khalil asked me to call you and let you know that he was arrested and on his way to the County jail.

Nadine took a deep breath.

"Thank you for calling! I will look into things." Nadine hung up quickly.

Cadence thought for a moment.

"She didn't even ask who I was! Or maybe she knows who I am?" Cadence shook her head as a way to remove her current thoughts. She had bigger things to think about like How do you do a bid with a dude in jail.

Cadence began new thoughts. "I don't know the first thing about jail. Heck I'm a lame. Why do they even call it a bid anyway?"

Cadence didn't know how this thing was supposed to go, but she knew she would figure it out!

One thing she knew was that she was intelligent.

Her intelligence was undeniable and she knew she could research and ask questions to get the answers she needed to make sure she was there for Khalil.

Cadence decided she needed to enlist help.

She thought to herself.

"Who can I trust? Who can help me through this?"

Cadence thought her best bet would be to rock with the people closest to Khalil.

Cheese and Tommy!

Cheese was like Khalil's right hand man, and Tommy was an older more sophisticated dude from the block who probably had better advice than Cheese.

She thought this would be the best of both worlds.

Cadence called Cheese even though it was early in the morning she knew that if she called him he would assume something happened and answer.

She scrolled through her text messages desperately searching for Cheese's number. After looking for what felt like an eternity she finally stumbled upon his number.

She pressed send and dialed Cheese's number.

The phone rang four times and went to voicemail.

"Man!!"

She thought to herself no answer.

Maybe he's looking at the phone like why is she calling me this late it must be an accident.

Cadence thought it would be best to try and call again just to make sure he knew it was an emergency.

Ring. Ring. Ring.

Cadence frantically said hello after receiving an answer, but there was no response.

"Hello! Hello! Cheese?"

Cadence stopped talking and listened intently instead.

She heard multiple voices of people she didn't know, but she definitely heard Cheese.

She pressed her ear to the phone closer as if it would assist her in hearing.

Muffled words crept through the signal lines of the phone.

Cadence began to think Cheese accidentally answered in his pocket until she heard a loud slamming sound as if the largest encyclopedia in the world had been slammed on a desk in an empty room that echoed.

Immediately after the bang came a loud ass

"TELL US WHAT YOU KNOW CHEEEEE-SE!!!"

Cadence pressed the phone even closer to her ear as if to make it a permanent part of her head, but all of a sudden the clarity of the call came through like someone removed a muzzle from over the phone.

Cadence's heart raced as she listened.

Then a light bulb came on!

Cadence quickly put her phone on mute to ensure that her background didn't alert the callers on the other line that someone was on the phone.

"CHEESE what's it going to be?"

We know all about the Dirty Dozen and their "beef" with 9339 you willing to go down for that?"

Cadence looked puzzled.

"Was this Cheese's interrogation?"

"How did his phone get answered?"

"What is going on here?"

Cadence knew hanging up wasn't an option so she remained alert and listened attentively.

There was a long silence and a deep sigh.

"You know where I'm from snitches get stitches and I ain't no snitch Cheese exclaimed."

Cadence was relieved!

She knew that Khalil was the best judge of character and he wouldn't have anyone around him that wasn't down with the team, but more importantly a man that would stand on his own.

Cadence heard another unfamiliar voice of what she now assumed to be a Chicago Police Officer.

"Cheese! Cheese! Cheese! Khalil's little project. His shadow in these streets. The number 2 guy. The guy who gets the "leftover" girls. The boy who gets the product rationed to him like a kid. The dude with no Mama. The one who couldn't handle the BOSS spot if it was handed to him, because he's just the trusty sidekick."

Wow!

They are laying it on thick!

That's absurd the things that they are saying to this dude Cadence thought.

Chicago Police are so dirty, and where are they even getting all of this information from anyway? They must be watching these dudes or something.

When I see Khalil I'm going to have to let him know something ain't right! Cadence began rehearsing the conversation with Khalil in her head.

She had completely blown off what the officers had said, because she knew Cheese was solid.

Her makeshift conversation was interrupted by

"I ain't nobody's trusty sidekick!"

Cadence rooted Cheese on in her head

"That's right, tell them Cheese!"

There was a long silence.

Cadence continued to cheer Cheese on because he was handling them like a champ.

Her cheerleading session was interrupted by Cheese's voice

"I ain't have nothing to do with what went down!"

OMG!!!!

Thought Cadence.

Cadence's heart began to race even more drastically now!!!

"I know I said tell them Cheese, but not LITERALLY!!!

What is this dude doing!

Cadence listened even more intently now.

She heard Cheese's voice begin up again.

"It was."

CLICK!

The next thing Cadence heard was the dial tone.

Did she accidentally hang up?

She moved her face and looked at the phone.

She didn't hang up, she was hung up on!

Just as Cheese was about to start singing like a canary or was he!

What was he about to say next?

Cadence was baffled and didn't know what to do!

She thought about calling Tommy, but her gut told her NO!

It seemed like Cheese just folded like the cleaners so could she trust him or Tommy, or anyone for that matter.

Chapter 18

The one thing Khalil KNEW was about to transpire was that he was DEFINITELY going to jail if he didn't get to the 9339 dudes and make some things happen.

He knew for certain that you couldn't go to jail if there was no one to press charges.

Khalil didn't want to get rid of the 9339 dudes, because he knew they would automatically be looked at as the assailants, and in reality he knew they didn't deserve that fate.

What he wanted was someone to go holler at the 9339 boys and try to pay them to play the game the way it went, but who could he have do it.

Most of the Dirty Dozen members that he trusted were locked up with him. LB, Ralph, and Cheese were all on their way in a patty wagon to the County in the next hour.

Khalil went through his mental rolodex picking out two cards: His Lawyer Mr. G and Betty.

Mr. G was the top defense lawyer in Chicago he could BEAT almost any case before him, or get you the least possible time appointed to you. He was a lawyer that was connected!

He knew other lawyers and police officers, but most importantly he knew Judges.

He came from a family of law. His father was a top attorney and his mother was a Judge. His brother was the former chief of police in Burbank, and his sister was the newly appointed head of the Cook County correctional facilities.

He was the GOAT of law, but those connections came with a hefty price tag.

Khalil plunged deeper into his thoughts!

He knew he had about $5,000 cash in the house, but he just re-uped on the work and passed it out on credit.

Majority of the street dudes did a lot of stunting!

They would flex to the chicks and other street dudes like they were holding that bag, but couldn't afford to pay for the work upfront.

They ALWAYS needed to be fronted and always had some type of sob story to go along with it.

Khalil was sick of it, but he knew it was how he made his money!

So he fronted them and kept a tab, because when they brought the money it was ALWAYS in pieces.

"This was a bad time to get bumped. I got a good $20,000 out here floating around, but people so faulty they operate on "Out of sight out of mind" so he knew he would only see about $5,000 of that money.

"That should carry me until the third court appearance. I need to make something happen by then. I can't count on nobody to come through with this lawyer bag.

If I can get to them dudes and get them paid I should be on my way out by the third appearance.

Khalil's thoughts shifted to Betty.

Betty was a girl he dealt with back in the day that was still his homie.

She knew a lot of people and happened to be the girlfriend of one of the 9339 boys.

"If I can get Betty to talk to them and tell them it was all just a misunderstanding and we will pay them if they don't show up in court we should be all---."

Line it up inmates.

It's time to load this patty wagon.

"You are now officially property of the Cook County Department of Corrections."

The new captives all lined up in a single file line that was longer than the line at the Aide office on 63rd when it was approaching Memorial Day.

Their heads were low and there was a slowness to their walk as if walking slower would prolong their fate.

Khalil looked around for Ralph, Cheese, and LB, but he hadn't seen them yet.

Khalil did a quick assessment of people to see if they would all make it, and according to his calculations they would.

The men started to stuff into the patty wagon and he finally spotted someone:

Ralph! He gave a head nod as to say what's up and kept moving back into the patty wagon.

"K! K!" Khalil turned slightly to his right and saw LB.

He gave him the same head nod of acknowledgment and moved to his spot.

He sat slowly and surveyed the other people in the patty wagon.

He looked around and noticed he hadn't seen Cheese.

He figured maybe he just overlooked him, and when they filed out at the County he would see him.

Khalil moved his thoughts to something more important.

"How was he gonna make it through this bid?"

He knew he had to assemble a team.

It was his strategy!

He knew one person couldn't do everything so if he had multiple people in place most things could get done.

He really didn't have any bros out in the street that he could trust to stand on their word, but he did have Nadine, his five sisters, and Cadence.

They would be able to hold him down!

He knew it would be a long ride, he also knew how much they loved him so it would all pan out.

As the patty wagon took off it felt like it was the beginning of a Nascar race.

The forward acceleration gave all the inmates and initial whiplash.

Unable to brace themselves due to being handcuffed everyone flew forward the weakest of the crowd hitting the patty wagon floor.

In that moment Khalil quickly looked if one of the three who fell were Cheese.

Still NO Cheese.

Khalil shook his head and thought to himself here we go!

He sat back and braced himself for the ride!

Not only the patty wagon ride, but the one his life was about to send him on.

WE WOULD LIKE TO PRESS CHARGES WE ARE VICTIMS OF A ROBBERY WITH A GUN!

Prior to walking into the station 9339 boys sat in the car after being robbed discussing the previous events.

"Man! They could have killed us" said the leader.

One of the other members chimed in:

"I told ya'll we shouldn't have been going back and forth with them in the first place. We are catholic school boys! We are from an entirely different world. They are from the streets! They do street stuff period!"

The leader looked at the member and said "You sound like a fan."

The boy lowered his eyes and then his head until another member stepped up.

"He's right! YOU are in some imaginary competition that you have drug us all into! We ain't trying to fight or die over none of this mess. They are STREET we are NOT! We are in two different lanes. We have to do stuff our way. They can have those girls and whatever claim to fame they want! We live good lives, with money, and active parents' stuff they could never have!!!"

The previous member raised his head, gained a little confidence and replied: EXACTLY!!

The leader of the crew listened to it all, but his personal vendetta ran so deep all that he heard was to do things their way and to stay in their lane.

The Dirty Dozen played street games, but they were clean cut so they played police games.

He thought for a moment about the repercussions of going to the police. "Well, they would all be out the way so we wouldn't have to worry about them anymore." What about their other guys?" As he answered himself he knew he had to be a tad bit crazy, but he had to think this all the way through.

"They would probably be scared to touch us because they wouldn't want to go to jail either! We could always rely on our boy Cheese to help us out anyway! We have been super cool since back in the day at school!

He's been rocking with us since the beginning and when the situation just played out he ain't even ride for them. His loyalty doesn't reside with them! I don't know fully if it's with us either, but he stayed in the car so he must be rocking with us!

We can have him keep the rest-----BRO!!!

His thoughts were interrupted by one of the members.

"What's the plan! They just robbed us and took our stuff! I think we should go holla at them and smooth things over. Tell them they can keep that stuff, and we don't want any smoke!"

The leader fumed: see he was a fake gangsta and he wanted to make a name for himself by any means necessary.

He had a faulty illusion that this couldn't end in death so he pressed the issue to the max.

The leader spoke up with a roar like Mufasa speaking to his tribe.

"I have listened to what you guys have been saying and what I have taken from it was that we need to play our own lane. Our lane is clean cut and involves doing things with REAL justice. We are going to the police station and pressing charges!"

"I AM NOT GOING TO THE STATION PRESSING CHARGES ON THEM!!!!! ARE YOU OUT OF YOUR FUCKING MIND THEY ARE GOING TO KILL US FORREAL!!!"

Calm down exclaimed the leader.

I've thought it through. Listen, if we go to the police they are out of our hair! I'm sure the gas station has cameras so they can't say we were lying! I know they ALL have to have backgrounds so it won't be their first offense they will be gone for some YEARS, and we can take over like it's supposed to be.

A couple of the members nodded in agreement.

They outspoken one who had the most sense spoke up

"AND WHAT ABOUT THE REST OF THEM?"

Everyone's focus shifted back to the leader.

We have Cheese for that!

Everyone looked confused!

Cheese was just with the people that robbed them.

The leader knew what everyone was thinking so he spoke on it.

"I know you all are saying to yourselves wasn't Cheese just with the dudes that robbed us?"

Yes he was! But did he help? NO.

Hasn't he been cool with us since school?

We rock with him on the courts, we see him at the club, and we even converse with him from time to time!

He showed more loyalty to us by not doing anything then he did to them.

I don't know if he's totally rocking with us, but he's definitely not totally rocking with them either.

When we press charges we leave him OUT of it!

He will be even more indebted to us!

His loyalty will totally shift and since he's the man over there like he told us he will be able to call the rest of the soldiers off!"

The outspoken one felt outraged

"YOU MUST BE CRAZY I'M NOT GOING TO ANYBODY"S STATION IF HE WASN'T ROCKING WITH THEM WHY HE DIDN'T TELL THEM TO STOP?"

Everything he said made sense, but his tone and delivery scared some of the other members.

The leader spoke with a sense of calm, but babbled with stupidity.

The members fell for what was on the surface and made a decision to press charges ALL except one!

The outspoken member spoke

"I can't do it ya'll! It makes no sense to me!"

The leader calmly replied "If you can't do this you ain't down with this crew!

Find you someone else to kick it with!

We are winning and we about to take them boys out!"

Cadence couldn't believe things were playing out the way they were.

Was Cheese a snitch?

It sounded like he was about to be, but could she be totally sure!

She wanted to tell Khalil, but did she want to put more pressure on him when he was already in a bind?

She needed to figure out how to help Khalil.

First things first she had to find out when his visiting day was.

She dialed the number slowly.

After half of a ring Cadence heard

"You have reached the Cook County Department of Corrections Inmate Information System for English Press 1."

Cadence pressed 1.

"To search for an inmate by booking number press 1."

Cadence pressed 1 again.

Cadence thought to herself I have no idea what his booking number is.

After pressing one the option popped up to enter by name.

Cadence entered the first four initials of Khalil's last name and the first four of his first name.

"You are calling about KHALIL Cadence pressed 1 for the operator to proceed she knew there wasn't another KHALIL out there in the world.

"Charge: ARMED ROBBERY". "DIVISION: 6 MEDIUM SECURITY" "VISITING DAYS: MONDAY & SATURDAY".

Cadence began to cry a little.

It was real Khalil was locked up.

She had always been there for him no matter what, and she tried to fix everything for him, but this she couldn't fix! She couldn't make this better all she could do was play her part and make it as light on him as possible.

Cadence knew she would ride with him all the way through.

She loved Khalil more than she loved herself and whatever she needed to do she would do!

Lost in her thoughts about what could be happening she snapped herself back to reality when she realized that it was Saturday and she needed to be making her way to the County for Khalil's visit.

It was 6:30 a.m.

Cadence had more than enough time to make it to the first visiting hours at 8:00 a.m.

She hopped in the shower quickly, threw on some clothes, and jumped in the car to make her ride to 26th and California.

She had never been to the County before so she decided to give herself enough time to make it there.

Driving down Lakeshore drive Cadence looked out upon the freely moving water thinking about the many nights her and Khalil took this same path in the car together just talking and riding.

The thought of him being away made her sick to her stomach.

When they were much younger Khalil got in trouble all the time, but because he was a minor he never really did any serious jail time, but his wrap sheet was as long as the distance on Lake Shore drive from Rainbow Beach to Ohio Street.

Cadence had a gut feeling that Khalil's time in the County was going to be a prolonged visit instead of a quick drop in.

Finally pulling up to the Cook County Department of Corrections for the first time was a tad bit scary.

The oatmeal brown bricks that were topped with bob wire were a bit over the top.

The County resembled a bland place of death and little did Cadence know the smell would hit her like death was awaiting her, but before she could even reach Division Six visitor check-in she was overwhelmed by the multitude of voices yelling their names through the small cracks of the windows in an attempt to solicit a visit.

"I.D. please" The guard stated before Cadence was even able to walk into the gates.

"No cell phones, no paraphernalia, no foul language, and no cameras."

Cadence was perplexed how can they police the visitor.

Cadence had her cell phone and handed it to the officer.

He looked at Cadence with a look of disgust.

"I am an officer of the law not a gatekeeper of cell phones. Take it back to your car or don't visit."

Cadence was taken aback by how rude the officer was and felt that if this was any indication of how this bid was going to go she was in for one heck of a ride.

Cadence briskly walked back to the car since it wasn't that far away. She actually had a great parking spot due to coming so early.

She walked back quickly to the "gatekeeper" in great anticipation of seeing Khalil.

The officer looked her over and opened his mouth to speak

"I.D."

Cadence began to get irritated with his antics.

He watched her walk to the car she knew this, because she watched him watch her. It was so early that there were no other visitors present yet.

Cadence played his game.

She didn't need any reason not to be able to see Khalil.

"No cell phones, no paraphernalia, no foul language, and no cameras."

Cadence nodded her head in agreement.

The officer continued.

"Walk down, make a right turn at the building and enter the first door."

Cadence almost wanted to run, she needed to see Khalil so bad. She used her long legs to take big strides, and finally made it to the door. She opened the oversized door and before entering there sat a guard.

"I.D."

Cadence wanted to scream.

She thought to herself how could I have loss my idea from "gatekeeper number one to the walk to gatekeeper number two."

She reached for her I.D. with such disgust she knew that the guard could feel her aggravation.

The guard looked Cadence over and spoke

"Go to the counter and tell the guard who you are here to visit."

Cadence looked around and the oddly painted orange walls. The orange in conjunction with the bland oatmeal cream convinced Cadence that they were trying to make inmates and visitors depressed.

Cadence realized that the place smelled as if every inmate had missed shower day and decided to play ball.

Division 6 was hot and the big metal fan to the right of the visitor check in counter was no help at all. It blew hot air and pushed the smell around terribly.

Cadence finally approached the counter and the guard said "Who are you here to see?"

Cadence said Khalil King.

The guard looked over her glasses as she typed into an ancient computer system. It was taking so long to make it to see Khalil it felt as if the officer had typed each letter one by one in an attempt to slow her down. The officer then picked up an old oatmeal bland colored phone that matched the depression of the walls exactly with a long tangled spiral cord and said

"Visit for Inmate King, Khalil".

Cadence thought for a minute.

King Khalil.

That had an amazing ring to it! She had never flipped his name around, but it resonated in her spirit, because to her Khalil was a King. She sat there basking in the thought of Khalil and him being the King that he is.

"HAVE A SEAT AND WAIT FOR HIS NAME TO BE CALLED!"

The officer yelled, interrupting Cadence's thought process and snapping her back to reality.

The waiting room was slowly starting to fill and as soon as Cadence was about to lower to sit in the seat "Khalil King."

Cadence stopped mid-squat and walked to the front.

"GO RIGHT"

Cadence went to the right and saw a long row of thick glass that had a yellow stain from never being cleaned or changed.

She looked at the gas station speaker that was placed in the middle that made you sound as if you were Dark Vader. Cadence looked all the way to the end of the room and saw Khalil sitting with his half of smile and his Kingly essence.

Even in the constraints of a jail visiting room the aura of who he was deemed undeniable.

Cadence sat down and put her face to the Dark Vader speaker, but was taken aback by the atrocious smell.

The metal piece with slits smelled as if every person who had ever came into the facility blew their breath in that place and a piece of it stayed. It was beyond foul, but she tried to chuck it up for Khalil.

Khalil however was a master of observation so he peeped that she was new to this and laughed out loud.

Cadence moved back to the stain glass window with the breathy metal piece and softly asked what's so funny?

Khalil replied: You! What's up?

Cadence thought to herself, because she was a true over thinker by nature.

"How can he be asking me what's up in this jam?"

Cadence thought about her next words.

She wanted to tell Khalil about hearing Cheese, but she was very cautious about the things that she told him.

There was no going back with Khalil.

Everything was a GO!!!

As soon as Cadence began to speak Khalil interrupted her "Man Joe have you seen Cheese?

He ain't in here and I'm trying to figure out how that played out?"

Cadence sighed a breath of relief.

"Yeah I knew you were arrested, because I was calling Cheese to tell him about you. I kept calling and got no answer. I finally called back and the phone randomly picked up, but he never said hello. In the background I could hear the police interrogating Cheese, and right before what sounded like him tricking on you the phone mysteriously hung up!!!"

Khalil sat back for a moment to process the information.

He knew he didn't have much time, but he made a mental note and moved back to the glass.

"Cadence I just need you to be there."

Cadence thought to herself why would I ever leave him?

But what she didn't know was the part of the game when people die or go to jail the stuff hits the fan FORREAL.

Cadence told Khalil she loved him and she would always be there for him.

Khalil replied "Alright shorty."

"Put some money on your phone and ride down on the block in front of the Cut and tell Chance I'm in here he will tell you what's next."

Cadence had so much to say, but saw a guard come to the opening and say something.

Khalil's head turned and she could see him give a head nod.

Khalil looked back to Cadence and said "They are calling me. I gotta go!"

Cadence wanted to cry.

That wasn't even 30 minutes, Khalil, she exclaimed loudly.

Khalil saw the hurt in her eyes and he was hurt too.

Only reply he could muster was "I'm on these people time now!"

He slowly got up and put his hand to the yellow stained glass and began to walk away.

Cadence choked back the tears, wiped her face, and proceeded to walk to the waiting room which was packed to the brim.

She looked around not noticing anyone in particular then she heard "Khalil King".

Cadence felt winded for a moment she looked around and saw 3 females walk toward the guard.

The guard seemed to sort out who was next, but Cadence was sorting out what was happening.

She looked at the faces vaguely remembering seeing a few, and started to doubt what she thought she shared with Khalil.

Leaving Cadence at the visiting window was hard for Khalil.

He actually really loved the girl, but just didn't know how to show it or let his guards down.

"Emotions get you killed, he thought."

Walking down the hall back to the cell he refused to look back at her; he knew he was going to have to be strong during this bid.

He thought about the conversation and what Cadence had said about Cheese he knew he had some ill-will toward him, but what he didn't know was how deep it ran.

Obviously it was deep enough to trick!

Khalil thought he had groomed Cheese for the street life instead he had put a clown fish in the sea with sharks.

Khalil however played Chess not Checkers so he would find a strategy to use this opportunity to help free himself and the guys.

He could use Cheese to talk to the 9339 dudes and hopefully resolve all of the drama before it even reaches the judge.

Khalil was set on going back to cell when he got in the back room his name was called again.

He figured that it was Nadine, but when he looked out he saw a chick from the hood he had slid on a couple of times.

One of the cool guards slid on him with a smirk and said

"It's gonna be a long day playa it's 2 more after that and it ain't even 9:00 a.m. You must be the man."

Khalil gave a brush of chuckle not to be disrespectful, because he didn't want any C.O. smoke, but enough to say "I ain't with the mess."

Khalil wasn't impressed by the visits though.

He knew the game and how it was to be played. Everybody started out good in the beginning, but who would stand the test of time?

He put on his smile and went to charm the people.

Throughout every visit strategizing how he can use this person to make it through this bid, and were they even worth the trouble.

12 visits later it was finally Nadine.

Nadine walked in with a sense of hurt.

She was so concerned about her baby boy she didn't know what to do.

Khalil's heart sank when he saw Nadine.

He knew she was coming, but he didn't know facing her would be so hard.

The last thing he ever wanted to do was disappoint her.

Nadine sat in front of her only son, and Khalil began to speak.

"Ma. We only got into a fight with these scary dudes, and now they are pressing charges saying......Nadine put up her hand to stop Khalil.

This ain't my first rodeo Khalil.

"I know how I may seem to you now, but I've been with your father my WHOLE life. I have a lawyer already lined up for you! He's the best to ever do it! He has beaten some very high profile gang-related cases so this is his line of business. He will be to see you Monday morning. Hopefully we can get the case thrown out, but for now you are going to have to sit and wait it out."

"Know it's just Satan Khalil. He knows your heart and he can't break you. You gotta stay strong.

Khalil shifted his body weight back and chuckled on the inside of himself in amazement.

He knew Nadine was solid, but this was a whole new level of solidity.

Kaleb was a mastermind in picking Nadine.

He molded and shaped her to the T. The pressure he put her through produced the diamond that Khalil saw before him. Nadine was an all-around winner and there was no denying that.

Khalil felt beyond lucky to have her as a mother and proud that his father had took the time to make her who she was.

After 13 visits he finally felt a sense of relief.

As long as he had Nadine he knew this would be an easier ride.

He knew she was right, it was a test, and the last thing he would ever do was fold.

Cadence slowly proceeded to walk out of Division 6 and began to start overthinking as she often did.

"Why were there so many girls there? Where did they come from? What were they doing there?"

As Cadence swiftly walked down California to her car she tried to push the thoughts out of her mind.

She had business to handle and couldn't let her thoughts get the best of her.

She had to get over East and meet Chance in front of the "Cut" to handle whatever business Khalil had sent her that way for.

She hopped in the Emerald green Sunfire and proceeded to Lakeshore Drive.

Cadence let the windows down and enjoyed the scenery on her ride back to the block.

She hoped that that first visit with Khalil was no indication of how this whole thing would play out.

The ride to the County felt like an hour because of the anticipation of seeing Khalil, but the ride back East took what felt like 5 minutes.

Cadence slowed down to park in front of the "Cut" which was ingeniously given the name, because of the ability to skip blocks by cutting through the opening that had a background of watered down mustard colored townhouses that lead to a cul-de-sac that opened to a larger street and train tracks.

The "Cut" had allowed many guys to elude the police, many dudes to escape their girl and side chicks, and was an amazing dip spot for the work. It was a multi-purpose place for the block. At any given second, minute, hour, or day you would find someone standing in front of the "Cut".

Cadence observed the scene as she often did when driving anywhere, but she was really looking for Chance, because if she didn't see him she didn't want to make the stop!

But true to nature Chance was standing in front of the "Cut" like always.

Cadence parked and proceeded to get out of the car.

Chance tall in statue stood in front of the "Cut" in a white wife beater and denim shorts.

Chance wasn't alone.

He was accompanied by Scars and Rafiki.

It was early so the old heads stood on post until the younger guys woke up.

Scars was an old head from out of town. He was solid and always encouraged the guys to express themselves through rap. You could find him on the corner in front of the mailbox. He dubbed this space the "Corner of Thought." He would hold rap sessions and mini battles giving the younger guys an outlet through bars.

While Rafiki took a different approach.

He was an old head in his lane getting to the money. He wanted the younger guys to shine! He could often be seen giving out his car, his chain, or some cash to aid in their shine. Rafiki was all about the glow of it, as long as your glow didn't out shine him things were all good in the hood.

Chance began to walk away from the entourage and looked at Cadence and smiled pointing to himself as if he was asking if Cadence wanted him.

Cadence replied by nodding her head and Chance proceeded to walk towards her.

Cadence began to speak, but Chance interrupted her and started to speak first.

"You know you're the one right. It's always been you! I told him you were the one and he knows it too!"

Cadence gave an uncomfortable chuckle not believing a word Chance uttered, because she had just left the County and encountered 3 females visiting Khalil.

Also, she knew dudes would say anything to help their guy look good.

Cadence attempted to change the subject, but Chance flowed the conversation.

"You need to call 773-431-0133. Ask for Cody or Tucson. They are brothers so you can talk to either one."

Cadence was confused.

She had never heard of Cody or Tucson in all the years she had been with Khalil.

Chance sensed her confusion and continued.

"They are the Ace in the hole. Cody and Tucson lived with Khalil and his mother off and on for years when they were younger. They will tell you what's next. They have access to some things and can tell you what to do until you talk to Khalil."

Cadence remembered that she needed to figure out how to put money on her phone so she could talk to Khalil.

Cadence got out of her thoughts and said "Thank You Chance!"

Chance replied "You got this! Remember you are the one!"

Cadence smiled and turned to walk toward the Sunfire.

Cody was a cool, kind-hearted gentleman. He would treat the janitor with the same respect that he would treat the CEO. He could often be found going out of his way to show how real he was not to prove a point, but he firmly stood by the mantra "Do unto others as you want done unto you!" He had an aura about himself that was undeniable. He could take the most insecure, chubby, unattractive female and make her feel like a crowned Miss America beauty queen with his genuine heart. He was one of a kind, a diamond in the rough.

Tucson on the other hand was a mastermind at using people to his advantage. If you didn't fit his bill then there was no use for you to him. He was self-less in some regards, but always made sure to put himself-first. People were chess pieces to be moved in his game for forward advancement. His heart wasn't totally cold though he had it in him to be kind-hearted like his younger brother, but life had shaped him in a way that pushed him to react the way he did.

Cadence wondered why Khalil didn't use the people whom she assumed were closer to him to conduct his business.

There was Mikey, Big Boy, or Jabar. They all had spent endless time with Khalil and were a part of the Dirty Dozen so she didn't quite understand.

Cadence then thought back to Chance and how he explained them as the "Ace in the Hole."

When she thought about the concept of the "Ace in the Hole." She realized that its purpose was to be hidden from the naked eye but assume the position of the highest of all rank.

Cadence took a moment to appreciate Khalil's thought process.

He was Mister Miyagi of the game making sure he was always 10 steps ahead of everyone.

Cadence picked up her phone and dialed "773-431-0133".

She listened intently.

The phone rang for what felt like two minutes.

Finally the phone stopped ringing and Cadence heard a dead silence.

Cadence looked around her car in extreme confusion and then she heard "YOOOOO!!!"

Cadence was taken aback and began to softly utter words. "Can I speak to Cody?"

"Who is this?"

The male voice replied sounding a bit like he was concerned who would be looking for him.

Cadence began to speak.

"This is Cadence. Khalil told me to give you a call."

"Ayyyeee replied the male voice on the other end. The demeanor of the voice changed from confusion into what sounded like the biggest Kool-Aid smile that could have ever existed.

"I've been waiting on you to call. How are you? You holding up?"

Cadence was confused by the questions seeing as how she never dealt with anyone in jail before so she blindly replied

"I'm good."

Cadence was unsure of who she was even speaking with because the unidentified male voice never gave his identity.

She was just about to ask if this was Cody when the male voice proceeded to talk.

"That's good! This is Cody. You can meet me at 2610 E 72nd Street in about an hour."

Cadence knew that an hour of street time meant two, but she was willing to give Cody the benefit of the doubt on their first encounter.

"Cool Cadence replied I'll be there."

Cadence hung up the phone and drove home.

She needed to figure out how to get money on her phone to receive Khalil's calls so she could get her directions straight from him.

Chapter 19

Khalil laid in the cot-sized bed as the locks popped for early morning breakfast.

He thought to himself "How did I get here?"

He took the swift walk to the dayroom for what the county assumed to be a high quality breakfast.

The oatmeal was plain and thick enough to choke a toddler, the eggs were questionable between the flat egg they serve for breakfast at Chicago Public Schools and some form of being scrambled, and beans that they didn't want to throw away from the night before, because at the core jail was a business and its all intents and purposes was not for rehabilitation, but to make money NOTHING MORE AND NOTHING LESS.

Khalil despised eating the garbage that they served.

He only ate enough not to starve.

One scoop of oatmeal, a square of their version of eggs, and a carton of milk was his daily portion of breakfast food.

Khalil tossed his tray and walked toward the phone line.

A loud voice abrupted out of nowhere "On The New!!!"

Khalil dropped his head, because he knew what type of lame mess came next.

"On them Mikes!" "Where you from? Who you wit?"

Khalil replied "You can get on these Mikes as long as you ready for everything that comes with them, and I'm from C-block! I'm ABK I ain't wit NOBODY PERIOD!!!"

The voice continued to shout "How you from over there! Who you know? You know Chance, Rafiki, Scars, or Tommy?"

Khalil took a moment to process.

"This dude validates being from over there by knowing another person? This has got to be a bunch of bullshit! "I know all them! I'm still ABK!" replied Khalil.

The voice now had a face beginning to emerge.

The slim Mexican walked forward and looked Khalil up and down!

He looked him dead in the face and said "NEWTRON ON DECK!!!!"

Khalil didn't even feel like fighting, but he knew what came with this.

If you didn't claim a set they figured you were weak.

Khalil was anything but weak and could by far beat anybody with his hands, or anything else for that matter.

He was like the Incredible Hulk!

One fact about Khalil there was no talking!

If it's time to get busy it's time to get busy.

He will discuss the details later.

Khalil knew what time it was!

As soon as the word "DECK" left Mexico's mouth Khalil landed a right then left punch straight to his jaw. The punches came so swiftly all you heard was the air blowing pass.

Mexico shifted to the left then shifted to the right.

He wobbled forward with what seemed to be noodles for legs, and then he fell face first into a breakfast tray.

The silence that was in the County for the swift second that punches were landed was as if every inmate were pupils in a library.

Then out of nowhere noise erupted "OOOOOhhhhhhhh."

Khalil didn't bathe in the false glory of knocking Mexico out.

It was actually out of his character to behave in such a way.

He never preyed on the weak!

It was against his philosophy of life.

He knew Mexico was weak the moment he opened his mouth from amongst the crowd, and not face to face like a real man would, but Khalil also knew an example had to be set, because you couldn't just do anything to Khalil and get away with it.

For every action there is a reaction!

Khalil proceeded to go to the phone line.

Along his walk lost souls poured beside him trying to rub elbows with the new proclaimed "King of the Dormitory."

Khalil was unbothered.

He gave nonchalant head nods and imaginary pulls of the Big Rig chain as a way to bypass the flunkies.

The last thing Khalil wanted or needed was a circle of some fly by night county bums.

He finally made his way to the phone line and approached the dude on the phone.

"I got next?"

Khalil both stated and asked at the same time!

Dude replied with half of his body facing Khalil and one ear to the phone

"There's a deuce in front of you bro!"

He proceeded to point out the two inmates that were next in line to use the phone in front of Khalil.

Khalil took a mental note and went to sit in the corner of the dayroom in an attempt to be by himself.

"I need to get Cadence on top of the business so I can try to get out of this jam, or at least lessen the effects of the jam I got myself into with these dudes that don't think pass go. They should have known better than to play with them square dudes from Catholic school, but........Khalil's thoughts were interrupted when he shifted his attention to the phone line.

He noticed that the first dude was off the phone and the next dude up was on the line.

There was one more in front of him and he was next.

Khalil got up and proceeded to walk back toward the phone line as a way to non-verbally say that he was reclaiming his spot in line.

Khalil walked, being very aware of his surroundings.

He was fresh off of knocking Mexico out and he didn't know if that came with some retaliation, what he did know was to be aware meant to be alive.

Khalil stepped to the front of the line because he was next.

The inmate standing in line looked annoyed with Khalil, because he thought that he was cutting the line.

Khalil stared him down, because he could tell dude had an issue, but he was so weak he wouldn't speak up; he would only give off a feminine attitude in an attempt to get Khalil's attention so he would address the situation.

Khalil ignored him totally and went forward with being next in line.

He picked up the phone and turned his head to the side because of the obnoxious smell of breath that engulfed the phone.

"Finally!!" Thought Cheese with a sinister chuckle.

"I finally have Khalil in a position to be out of my way! I'm really the man and played the background to this chump for way too long. He has all these dudes spooked for NO apparent reason. He has all these chicks lined up, and he plays continuous games with them, and he ain't running the crew like I would. I was built for this! Now it's my-----Cheeses' thoughts were interrupted by the vibration of his cell phone.

UNKNOWN CALLER....... Cheese took a moment he knew this could only be Khalil.

He took a deep breath and exhaled deeply as to rid himself of the hatred he was just spewing through his mind.

"HELLO!"

The prerecorded message began.

You have a collect call from an inmate at the Cook County Correctional Facility Press 1 to accept the charges.

Cheese proceeded to Press 1.

The recording continued.

Thank you!

You are now being connected.

"HELLO!"

Repeated Cheese.

Khalil came through the phone. "What's to it fam?"

Cheese paused for a moment.

He began to think to himself. "WHY is he asking me what's to it and calling me fam? Can he read my thoughts? Naw he can't read my thoughts! He ain't that cold. Does he know what I'm on?"

Cheese was on high alert! He knew he was beyond bogus, but he thought he was ahead of Khalil with his thought process. Was he overthinking?

"FAM!!! I said what's to it?" Khalil repeated himself with a little more assertiveness.

He knew Cheese was a fraud and he knew by now that the love he had for Cheese wasn't being reciprocated.

What he was trying to figure out was how deep did the hatred flowed.

Cheese began to reply.

"Nothing!" "Ain't Nothing up with me. I slid out the jam luckily now Imma be able to take care of the business for y'all from the outside. I'm glad one of us can stand on top of the business and the block while all of this is going down. I got you! What you need me to do?"

Khalil shook his head at the phone.

See Khalil was an observer of people and their behavior.

He played close attention to their word choices and body language.

He felt as if this was the true indication of who a person was as opposed to what they said or showed you.

Cheese had shown his hand to Khalil by saying he was glad one of us could stand on top of the business and block. It proved the point that he wanted to take over. Khalil proceeded at this point he knew he had to work with what he had.

"Yeah man you're right! I'm glad all of us aren't in this jam either. You know them 9339 dudes anyway so that will help us out. I got $5,000 at the crib. I want you to go holla at them and tell them not to show up at court. There is no case if there are no witnesses. I know we will probably have to sit a few months for the courts to continue the case, but after a while they will get tired of them not showing up, and drop it and let us up out of here!"

Cheese thought about it.

Khalil was right again.

If 9339 didn't show they would most definitely get out.

Cheeses' thoughts were interrupted by Khalil

"You think you can handle that fam?"

The operator interrupted: You have one minute remaining!

Cheese began to fume.

"See that's the probably he thinks everyone is less capable than him of doing things. Why couldn't I handle talking to some dudes I have in the palm of my hand? I'm the man!!! I can make anybody do anything! He is a fool! Doesn't he see I win! I'm not in jail! I'm really the mastermind! Smarter than he ever will be! I've been planting the seeds of hatred in the 9339 dudes heads all along. I've been telling them that they had more legit money than us, more chicks than the Dirty Dozen, and flyer clothes. I'm really the puppet master and now it's time for my ultimate move!! I'm going to run the Dirty Dozen! I'm going to run the block! I'm going to have all the girls, and I'm going to get all the money and stunt on

EVERYBODY!! ESPECIALLY KHALIL!!!! I'm Batman and he's ROBIN!!!"

Cheese put his plan to the side for a moment and uttered a reply; "I got you Khalil! I can handle that! I'm going to make sure you get...............

THANK YOU FOR USING SECURUS GOODBYE.

Cheese finished his statement after the phone hung up.

"I'm going to make sure you get: EXACTLY WHAT YOU DESERVE!!!!!

Cadence knew she was dealing with another street dude, but she decided to partially give Cody the benefit of the doubt.

He told her to meet him in an hour which in street time she knew meant two hours, but she decided to pull up to 2610 E 72nd street in an hour and a half.

Cadence pulled the Emerald green Sunfire in front of the court way and outside was standing a brown skin boy.

He seemed to be waiting on someone, and started to walk towards the Sunfire while Cadence perfected her parking.

He bent down into her open window and said

"Cadence what took you so long! I've been out here for 30 minutes followed by a small chuckle and the biggest kool aid smile that ever existed in this realm of the Earth.

His demeanor was one of pure joy! You could feel the essence of life exuding off of him.

He opened the Sunfire door and hopped in the front seat.

He could feel the confusion in Cadence's body language and proceeded to introduce himself.

"My apologies! I just hopped in your car without a formal introduction. I was wrong off back."

Cadence's look of confusion slowly began to dissipate.

"Now that's better! I'm assuming my apology was befitting since your growl has turned upside down!!!!

Cody exclaimed then chuckled a deeply rooted laugh that was almost contagious followed by that kool aid smile.

Cadence thought to herself I don't know how anyone could ever be mad at this dude his aura is too nice. He laughs and smiles at any given moment! Does he even have the capability of getting mad?

Cadence cleared her throat and began to speak.

" I..I..I should be the one offering you the apology. I should have been here on time, but you know street dudes operate on their own clock. So I thought your hour meant 2 hours so I actually thought I was coming early!"

Another deep chuckle erupted from Cody! His laugh made you want to laugh and his smile made you want to smile.

Cadence could feel his energy rubbing off on her!

The next thing she knew she was smiling and laughing also!

Cody began to speak "Off back, I'm different then these other street dudes. I operate by a code of honor and if I say something I stand on it! But let's get to the order of business. I have $5,000 dollars right here for you. You need to meet Mr. G the lawyer at Dunkin Donuts on 15th and Michigan. He is expecting you in 30 minutes now since you weren't on time."

Cadence didn't know how to take Cody saying that to her she began to put up her defense walls, but before she could he erupted in a chuckle and smile so deep she knew he meant no harm!!

"You need to tell Mr. G exactly what happened. You can tell him the truth, he works for you and he's good with us. Also let him know you will be Khalil's point of contact so whatever he needs as far as money let him know to contact you!"

Cadence began to look a little perplexed Cody continued

"Don't worry at that point you will contact me, and I will round up money off of the streets for you to give to the lawyer. Just a heads up this street money almost ALWAYS comes back short. Make sure you have some money on deck to be able to add to what's given to you. You can't completely rely on these dudes."

"Outta sight outta mind!"

Also remember no matter what you see or hear during this time remember

"You are the one!"

"Now get outta here before you're late to meet somebody else!"

Cody hopped out the car as quickly as he hopped in a popped his head back in the window and smiled

"Have a good one Cadence, off back!"

Cadence pushed her foot down on the brake pedal and proceeded to take the Drive north towards 15th street so she could meet Mr. G.

She looked over in the passenger seat where Cody had left the brown paper bag of money.

She made it her duty to always count money when people gave it to her just as a checks and balance system.

She pulled off of the drive at 47th and proceeded to pull in the parking lot of Walgreens.

She needed to do a quick count.

She opened the bag and saw all hundreds.

She thought to herself "This will be easy and quick."

Cadence began thumbing through the money like a money counter.

Her days working in the cash office aided in her ability to swiftly count money.

41, 42, 43, 44, 45, 46, 47.....48! 48 hundred dollar bills.

"THIS IS SUPPOSED TO BE $5,000!!!"

Cadence quickly remembered Cody's advice street money almost ALWAYS comes up short.

Cadence took a deep sigh and pulled over to Citibank to get $200 to complete the payment for the lawyer.

Cadence thought to herself: AND SO IT BEGINS!!!!!!

Chapter 20

Khalil reluctantly returned to his cell after a day filled with events beyond his belief he knew by now that Cadence had to be on top of the lawyer business for him, and that Cody had played his part to the fullest.

He made his way to the bottom cot and stretched his legs as far as the twin size mat would allow.

"How am I going to make this happen? I know I have to sit down, but the length of time is what is questionable at this point. My background is rather sketchy, but my lawyer is the best in town! If I can solidify 9339 dudes not showing up to court then I'm good. I'll probably be here a couple of months tops and they will let me out. I have to have Cheese and Betty work their number with 9339. It's really their little leader that they need to address. He is the one with personal vendetta. If I could just appeal to his emotions then maybe I could get him to stand down. If I wave the white flag and surrender whatever position it is he believes I'm holding it could make the situation the best possible outcome for all of us."

"My bad bro!"

Khalil's thoughts were disrupted by the vague apology that was offered by his cellmate as he attempted to excuse the foul odor he emitted from his body.

"It was the beans we had for dinner bro. They are killing me."

Khalil sat up from his semi-comfortable position and began to speak

"Correction. You're killing us!!"

"Dump and flush!"

The cellmate hopped up in his oatmeal attire and swung his feet to the front of the metal bunk.

He thought about the concept of dump and flush for the moment.

He was new to jail.

He just got caught up with the wrong crowd trying to have fun.

This was a whole new world for him.

He gazed around the room to answer the infamous statement dump and flush as if the graffiti ridden walls had answers that would escape the walls and float into the air to answer his burning question.

He sat there perplexed for a little bit longer as he continued to emit the raunchy odor.

Khalil now beyond irritation with his total disregard for the small space said

"DUMP and FLUSH!!!".

Cellmate knew this was now no longer a suggestion, but quickly escalated to demand.

He turned face forward to the metal bunks and slowly climbed down.

He made his way to the "restroom" which was a filthy toilet located in the corner of the room.

The brown rings of bowels from inmates of years stained the inside of the toilet.

The seat was barely hanging on by a hinge, and he thought to himself

"How do I comfortably relieve myself here?"

All I know is I better try.

Khalil hated this part of jail.

It was completely inhumane to make another person be in the same small living quarters with another as the removed defecation from their body.

No one should have to endure the grossness of this situation Khalil thought.

He took his white stained sheet and carefully balled it to perfection and placed it against the wall in his attempt to configure a makeshift pillow.

He then positioned himself in such a manner that only his feet hung off the too small cot mattress.

He then took the itchy oatmeal blanket and attempted to cover his entire body.

He chuckled to himself.

He knew that was a joke.

The itchy oatmeal burlap blanket wasn't long enough to cover much of anything.

"Who am I fooling?" Khalil thought.

The Cook County Department of Corrections does nothing to make you comfortable!

They give you what they HAVE to!

Khalil took the burlap blanket slab and covered his head in an attempt to remove his mind from his physical location.

Khalil had finally found a small pocket of peace when it was quickly disrupted by a loud grunt.

Cellmate had now found his own little pocket of peace.

He positioned himself on the broken toilet seat back hunched and eyes fixated on the bars.

He always sat like this at home in his lavatory.

It aided in the movement of his feces through his digestive tract.

He always had a slight problem with constipation, but jail food complicated issues even more.

To add insult to injury he had to make an odd grunting noise.

He didn't quite understand it himself, but it was part of his routine.

"Humf. Humf.Humf."

Khalil could no longer take the total disrespect for the unspoken jail house "rules".

He tossed his burlap slab to the side and turned his body to face the rather naïve cell mate that he was stuck with.

"Listen clearly you are new to this whole jail thing, but let me assist you with giving you the rundown of these unspoken jail rules.

Let's start with the most pressing issues first.

DUMP and FLUSH!!!

You do NOT by any circumstances get comfortable in relieving yourself of feces when we BOTH are in here.

You drop a dump.

Immediately flush it, and get off the can!

There are no weird noise making, time lapsed, concentrated bowel movements when we are both in the cell.

If you have to take a dump you need to take a peanut butter cap and put it in the lock when the pop the doors.

This will allow for our cell to stay open all day and you have the comfortability you need to relieve yourself, or you can do it in the alley.

Cellmate looked confused.

Khalil reluctantly continued.

The alley is the bathroom with no stalls in the dayroom. You know just the rows of toilets with no privacy.

You can drop your load there with six other dudes to watch you choose, but right now.

DUMP and FLUSH!!!!

I'll give you the rest of the game as it presents itself.

Khalil grabbed the itchy burlap slab and shifted his body back to the wall.

He laid on his makeshift pillow and thought

"I gotta get out this jam expeditiously!"

Cadence despised the thought of being late to meet Mr. G.

She knew he was a professional man with a multitude of things to do.

She also didn't want to give him any reason not to fully represent Khalil to the best of his ability.

The traffic driving down Indiana street seemed to be at a standstill this particular day and Cadences' frustration was beginning to get the best of her.

"Honk. Honk. Get out of the way! My God this is like driving Ms. Daisy. I can't believe how slow you're driving."

Cadence yelled out of her open window.

The driver seemed to take her words very personally, and began to intentionally drive slower to hinder Cadence from going wherever it was she thought she was going.

After ten blocks of road rage shenanigans Cadence found an opening to get from around the driver and be on her way, but not before she shot him the dirtiest look that she could fathom.

If looks could kill Spot News would be at the corner of that intersection making their report because Cadence would have assassinated him on the spot.

She was already 15 minutes late to meet Mr. G and she hated when she wasn't on point.

Especially, when it concerned Khalil!

Just as Cadence was about to escape into her thoughts she felt the slight vibration of her phone and looked down to see who could be calling her right now.

The screen read: TINY!

Cadence hadn't talked to Tiny in a couple of weeks and was curious as to what she had been up to.

She picked up the phone. "GIRL!!!"

Tiny erupted in laughter on the other end.

"I know. I know." Tiny began. "I have been super busy girl."

Cadence smacked her lips as if she was non-verbally telling her she didn't want to hear it, but Tiny continued anyway.

"I've been with my bay nonstop and I can't get enough of him."

Cadence knew that Tiny wasn't really the settling down type so for her to go M.I.A and to be calling someone her boo she knew it was something to all of it!

"Your boo?"

"Now Tiny you aren't the pet name, wrapped up in someone type of girl! Who's the mystery fella?"

Tiny sounded as if she was smiling immensely through the phone.

"Cadence I know I don't play any games with these dudes. My brothers taught me long ago that they all play too many games! I've never settled down because I've never found anyone worthy of my time or attention!" But Cheese! Cheese is different! He has a heart of gold! He loves me unconditionally! We share everything with one another. He's my best friend other than you!"

Cadence wanted so badly to be happy for Tiny, but she knew how much of a snake Cheese was.

She forced herself to fake a smile and told Tiny congratulations.

"I'm happy for you if you're happy!"

Tiny didn't need Cadence's approval, but was completely relieved that she was okay with it.

Cadence forced more to make Tiny feel comfortable.

"Maybe one day we can double date!!"

Tiny took a long pause.

The silence began to become deafening.

"Tiny what's wrong, why did you get so quiet?"

"Well Cadence I know this is none of my business, but you are my girl! I always try to stay out of people's mess."

Cadence interjected.

"WHAT IS IT?"

"Umm.. I overheard Cheese on the phone talking to some chick. They were talking about the details of Khalil's case."

Cadence shook her head.

"Tiny I'm sure there are plenty of chicks wanting to know about Khalil and the details to his case. Everybody is concerned about what's going on with him."

Tiny was tired of trying to beat around the bush and spare Cadence's feelings.

"Girl Khalil has a girlfriend! A Girlfriend who AIN'T you!!"

"GIRLFRIEND??? GIRLFRIEND????"

Cadence dropped the phone mid yelling girlfriend.

She had finally made it to her destination.

She pulled in front of the Dunkin Doughnuts.

She took a deep breath to gain her composure and locate her cell phone.

After fumbling for what felt like hours on the floor of the car she finally located the phone.

She could faintly hear Tiny screaming.

"Cadence are you okay?"

Cadence could fill the tears swelling up in her eyes. She tried to hold back the tears and remove the very large knot from her throat. At the essence of things she still had business to take care of.

Cadence could see Mr. G through the picture window at Dunkin Doughnuts. He continued to look at his watch, and she could tell he was becoming a tad bit impatient.

"Tiny what do you mean girlfriend?"

Tiny cleared her throat as if that would help soften the blow of what she was about to say.

"Girl Cheese was talking to the girl telling her all the details. More details than he has ever told anyone else. So you know me! I started asking questions. He finally told me after I interrogated him that the girl was Khalil's girlfriend. He said that they have only been together a couple of weeks, but they have been talking for a long time."

Cadence could feel the tears streaming down her face.

"After all of this!"

Cadence thought to herself.

Cadence wiped her face and began to speak.

"Thanks Tiny! I appreciate you girl! I'm about to go handle some business. I'll call you later."

"Are you okay Cadence?"

I've been trying to figure out how to tell you, but I just didn't know how!"

"I'm good Tiny! Thanks again! I gotta roll!"

Cadence hung up the phone.

She wiped her face.

Put on her big girl panties and exited the car.

She put on the fakest smile she could muster and walked in Dunkin Doughnuts to handle the business for Khalil amidst the rumors of his "girlfriend"!

Cheese decided it was high time to call a Dirty Dozen meeting with the heads of each area.

He wanted everyone to rest assured that money was still going to be made while Khalil was fighting his case.

Cheese called Jabar, Big Boy, Mikey, Reckless, and Rito.

He told them to meet him at the cut in 30 minutes so they could have a discussion.

The crew pulled up like clockwork eager to know what was going down with Khalil.

What Cheese didn't know was that Khalil never really tightly held the reins on any of the members of the Dirty Dozen. Every man was their own individual man getting to their own money in their own way! They were just basically a crew who decided to link up, because of common interests.

"I called us all here today to talk about how things are going to operate moving forward. I just wanted you guys to rest assured that I have things in place to make sure money will still be made while Khalil is fighting his case! Everything will operate as smoothly as it always has been if not better!"

Cheese continued on with his spill.

He never even noticed the look of confusion on the faces of the people before him.

Finally Reckless interjected.

"What the hell are you talking about FAM?"

Rito gave a head nod as to second Reckless' injection.

Cheese looked perplexed "What do you mean what am I talking about? I'm telling you what's about to happen next! I wanted y'all to know that y'all was going to still be good while Khalil is fighting this case. He put me in charge and I will make sure the day to day operations run smoothly!"

"IN CHARGE!"

Reckless was like a loose cannon waiting to explode at any given moment.

"What do you mean in charge? There is no other man in charge of me! I am my own man in charge of myself! I don't know what Khalil has told you, but this whole concept has me twisted." "Yeah I get my own money! I might occasionally cop from him, but it's nothing like what you are saying! Maybe you are the one tripping though, because I can't even see Khalil talking like that! This isn't even his character or style!" exclaimed Rito.

Mikey decided that he had had enough.

"I have no time for foolery! I got to get to the money Cheese. Hit me when you have some info about Khalil's case."

He jumped in his car and sped off.

Rito was fed up already too. He never really cared for Cheese anyway. He just respected him out of love for Khalil, but Khalil was off the scene and Cheese was clearly off of his square.

"Yeah me and Reckless are going to shoot back over to our side of town to get OUR OWN money! Tell Khalil to hit my line."

Reckless was ready to take off on Cheese, but opted against it.

He just gave him a look and got in the passenger side of the car with Rito and they too sped off.

Jabar and Big Boy stood still looking perplexed.

See these two were different.

They needed something to believe in and Khalil was their life line.

So if Khalil said Cheese was taking over.

Then Cheese was taking over!

Cheese knew he still had an audience in them so he continued with his misconstrued plan.

"We have the East Side on lock! All we have to do is continue the formula we know and make this money!"

Jabar and Big Boy began to light up!

Money brought the girls around and all they really wanted was them anyway.

Big Boy sopped up words like syrup on biscuits.

He believed everything Cheese said.

He was on board with the plan, and glad that Khalil was giving them the opportunity to make things happen in his absence.

Big Boy genuinely wanted to work hard for the Dirty Dozen.

He wanted to move up his "rank".

He knew with the improved social status came more girls and more money, and that's all he lived for at the moment.

Jabar on the other hand displayed a sinister smirk.

He had his own plan in mind.

He knew Cheese wasn't the best possible candidate to run the Dirty Dozen.

He could pick up on his character flaws, because they shared the same traits.

Self-centered, selfish, and lacked the capability to listen to another individual.

Basically, a know-it-all that knew nothing at all who never matured out of the stage of being egotistical.

However, Jabar didn't want the claim to fame of the Dirty Dozen.

He had his eye on a prize much more personal to Cheese.

"Now my plan is in motion. Forget Reckless and Rito! I never needed them anyway. If they think they can eat out on the streets without the Dirty Dozen let them try! I'm in charge now, and once you cross me there is no coming back. So they are done on these streets. DONE! DONE!"

"I do however need someone on my team that I can trust! Who can you really trust though?"

Look at me and Khalil.

Cheese raced through his mind on whom he could possibly bring in to help him bring his plan full circle?

Who could he allow to help him in running the Dirty Dozen that was pure enough not to try to take over what he was building?

Cheese thought for a moment.

While encompassed in his thoughts the phone began to buzz.

"Yeah Boo! What's up?"

"Hey Cheese" Tiny started reluctantly.

"What's wrong Tiny? What's to it I'm kinda busy right now!"

Tiny took a deep breath and continued

"I'm just going to spit it out! I told Cadence about Khalil's girlfriend. We were talking and, and she just needed to know!!"

"YOU DID WHAT??????"

"I can't believe you there is so much on the line for me right now! If I can't trust you, who can I trust? You are supposed to be my girl, and...."

Tiny interjected

"FIRST, you're going to watch your tone and talk to me in a respectful manner."

Secondly, Cadence has been my friend long before I met you! I love you, and we are in this together but I HAD to let her know!"

"Tiny I don't have time for this mess! You better figure out how to fix it, and fix it now!"

Tiny let out a sinister chuckle

"Boy get off my line! She stated and then immediately hung up."

"I don't need this right now! Khalil might be a lot of things, but a dummy ain't one. He's gonna start putting two and two together and I'm going to have to start watching my back. Tiny doesn't even understand how she just added fuel to an already well-lit fire. I need to put my plan more swiftly in motion. "

Who can I count on?

Cheese continued to run through the dudes he hung out with and finally had an epiphany.

MANOR!!!

MANOR is the man with the master plan.

Manor was a dude that Cheese had attended Catholic School with.

He was nothing like the 9339 dudes though he actually was a real one.

Manor was kind of tall, medium brown, and a live wire ready to pop off at any moment.

See Cheese had a way of getting himself positioned around real ones so he could live off of their life line.

Cheese had done the same thing with Khalil, but the difference between Khalil and Manor was the patience.

Manor possessed a heart of gold like Khalil, but he wasn't for NONE!!!

Khalil would let Cheese slide A LOT only in attempts to have him learn through the process.

Manor didn't care.

In his book you either had it or you didn't.

Cheese was a chameleon though.

He took Khalil's philosophies, mannerisms, and even fashion sense and adopted as his own.

He had fooled Manor over the years and Manor had no clue.

He thought he was in the company of a real one!

Cheese knew that Manor would bring some solidified experience to the table.

He was a lot like Khalil, but he was better because he knew nothing of Cheeses' shortcomings which made him easier to manipulate.

Cheese picked up his phone and proceeded to dial Manor's number.

The phone rang for what felt like an eternity before Cheese heard a loud "YOOOOO!"

"Manor what's to it my dude?"

Manor took a moment to catch the voice.

"Cheese what's up boy. You ain't hit me up in a couple of weeks. What have you been up to?"

Cheese thought about the best way to present the opportunity to Manor.

He thought for a moment.

What would Khalil say?

"Manor I have an undeniable business opportunity I want to holla at you about. You got some time today? I want to sit down with you?"

Manor answered rapidly.

"You know I always rock with the real! Where you want me to get up with you?"

Cheese replied. "Meet me at Hayes in 30."

"Alright my dude I'll see you there!" Manor responded.

Cheese put his key in the ignition and began to turn it to the right to crank the engine.

"I'm about to take the Dirty Dozen and the block to the moon! Nobody is ever even gonna remember Khalil! I'll make sure of it!"

Cheese pulled out of his park and cruised to Lake Shore Drive.

"This is going to be a breeze he thought to himself. I'm about to be the man!"

Chapter 21

"GIRLFRIEND!!!" Cadence tried to calm down before she stepped out of the car to meet the lawyer Mr. G.

"Deep breath Cadence."

She coached herself into pulling it together.

Cadence grabbed the door of Dunkin Doughnuts and faked a smile.

She made her way to the table where Mr. G had made himself comfortable and joined him across the table grabbing a seat

. "Hello Mr. G! My apologies for my tardiness."

Mr. G looked Cadence over and offered a quick smile.

He picked up his coffee cup and lifted it as a fake toast and nonverbal way to accept Cadences' apology.

Mr. G wasn't your typical lawyer.

He was highly connected and powerful.

His clients were the types that were usually guilty, but he had a knack about getting people off.

He also had this insane twitch that kind of made you nervous at first sight. It was so defined that it made his clients question if he could possibly represent them correctly, but his reputation for winning always preceded him so he usually didn't have a problem getting clients.

Mr. G had a 95% success rate at beating cases, and what he didn't beat he got you sentenced to the least possible amount of time for that particular crime. He won, because he knew the letter of the law, and wherever a cop, lawyer, or judge slipped he used it in his favor!

"Hello Cadence it's very nice to meet you! You're way prettier than I thought dealing with Khalil!"

Mr. G laughed at his own joke.

Cadence forced a smile.

"Well let me cut to the chase Cadence. This is going to be a hard case to beat. There is video and there are witnesses. I am going to try my best to win, but in a worst case scenario I will try to get Khalil the least possible sentence. The Cook County Department of Corrections is extremely overcrowded right now. Therefore, cases are being called very slowly. My clients that are incarcerated now are receiving court dates on average that are four months apart. I'm almost positive we will have a couple of continuances, and to just be straight forward Khalil is looking at minimum to be fighting in the County for at least a year!"

Cadence took a gasp of breath.

This is really happening she thought!

Mr. G continued.

"My initial fee is $15,000. This cost may increase as I get into the inner workings of the case. I understand you were supposed to give me a payment today of $5,000 dollars.

Cadence nodded her head in agreement and slid the brown paper bag across the table to Mr. G.

Mr. G continued his spill.

"I will work my angles and to try to ensure that Khalil is free. I have already requested that the case go before Judge Wavy. He is an awesome Judge that sentences people strictly according to the law. I have never witnessed him have a bad day and take it out on an inmate. In my 20 years of practice I have always found him to be fair and just. I have even witnessed Judge Wavy tell officers "It doesn't matter to me if he committed the crime or not. You did not do your duty of upholding the law and making a lawful search or arrest", and then he would dismiss the case. I believe Wavy is our best possible choice for a fair and just trial."

Cadence took it all in.

Mr. G who loved to talk proceeded.

"I will go and visit Khalil in a couple of days. I will get his side of the story and start trying to compile some evidence to help lessen the blow of the evidence in the case.

"I have a question."

Cadence started with a slightly shaky voice.

Between Khalil's girlfriend and this dampening news Cadence was ready to cry.

"What if the witnesses don't show up?" asked Cadence.

Mr. G shrugged his shoulders.

"I don't suggest you go knocking people off over this case."

Cadence laughed a little.

"I'm not going to knock anyone off. What if I just persuaded them not to show up!"

Mr. G stopped fumbling with his coffee and looked up at Cadence.

"Just keep your interactions with this group of people at a minimum. They are okay, but they don't want much for themselves. I get the feeling that this case is personal, and sometimes trying to convince someone to not show up can come back to haunt you. But theoretically if they don't show up it will definitely help with beating Khalil's case. It's not a sure thing though, because sometimes the State is so gung ho on sending people to jail that they will pick up the case even if the Plaintiff decides to have a change of heart. That is much further down the road though let's get through this first court appearance and see how things pan out. Khalil has to be in court next Friday at 10:00 a.m. It's always good to have family or friends show up to court. It shows the Judge that this is an individual that people care about."

Cadence nodded her head in agreement.

She was sure someone would be there, but WHO was the million dollar question.

Mr. G began to gather his things and stand up.

"Cadence it was very nice meeting you! I will see you in court next Friday. It is usually my policy to collect on the remaining balance at each court date so please bring $2,500 dollars with you at that time."

Mr. G extended his hand to Cadence.

Cadence stood up and reached to shake Mr. G's hand.

"Thank you for everything Mr. G!"

"You don't have to thank me! This is what I do!"

Mr. G quickly exited the Dunkin Doughnuts and disappeared swiftly around the corner.

Cadence flopped down in the chair.

She was exhausted from trying to focus on business and putting her feelings to the side.

She was crushed about Khalil and his "girlfriend"!

"I don't know what I was thinking. I thought WE were together. I thought WE were working towards something special. If he has a "girlfriend" why am I here meeting the lawyer? This makes absolutely NO sense. Is Cheese trying to sabotage our relationship through Tiny or is this true."

Cadence had a few days before she would see Khalil and ask him herself, but in the meantime she felt it would be best for her to pull back.

"It's one thing to be played by someone, but it's a totally different thing to play yourself!"

The locks popped on the jail cell.

It was time for the morning slop.

Khalil slowly trudged to the chow line

Breakfast was the worst time of day to Khalil.

They woke the inmates extremely early to eat and sent them back to the cells for three hours unless you had court.

Khalil had been in the County many times before, but it was never as overcrowded as this.

He knew his court date would probably take a while to come, but he hadn't seen Mr. G yet and that was concerning and unusual.

Khalil knew it was best to do his time and not worry about the world, because it would drive you crazy.

He couldn't help thinking about Cadence though.

He knew he owed it to her to be upfront and honest because she deserved that.

They were very close friends, and by all time and situations they had been through together one could assume that they were in a relationship.

Khalil had a reason for EVERYTHING he did.

He had been talking to the other girl for quite some time.

He knew what he shared with Cadence was solid, but he wanted to make sense of the other situation, and what better time to do it than when the situation was under pressure.

Khalil was a firm believer that "pressure busts pipes."

Khalil hoped that Cadence would understand and still remain his friend and stay in his corner, but if she didn't he knew what was for him was for him.

What Khalil didn't want was for Cadence to find out from someone other than him.

That would be a killer and he didn't want to break her heart like that!

In reality Khalil knew that being concerned with a woman was probably the last thing he should be doing.

From his experience women were not trustworthy. They will talk a good game, but that's all it usually is. Talk!

Khalil was ready to be upfront with Cadence and hoped it would all work out in his favor.

Lost in his thoughts Khalil began to weigh the pros and cons of telling Cadence even though he knew he really had no choice in the manner.

Khalil proceeded to indulge in his usual portion of breakfast when he heard a familiar voice "BROOOOO."

Khalil put his head on swivel and began to look around the dormitory.

He didn't see anyone he recognized.

Then BAM a breakfast tray was slammed on the table before him.

Oatmeal flew in the air and the County's rendition of toast hit the floor.

Khalil instantaneously got on attack mode. Khalil was ready for what he deemed to be war, but began to focus his eyes.

'RALPH???"

"What's to it Khalil?"

Khalil felt a little mind boggled.

"Ralph how did you get here?"

"They moved me man! I was getting into too much mess in that other division. I had talked to my girl and she told me the streets were talking and they said you were in this division. So when I found out I was coming down here I was good! Did you get in touch with a lawyer?"

Khalil was still baffled by the fact that he was in the same division with Ralph. It was good and bad. Ralph was his boy, but Ralph was a tweeker. He operated in his own world, one which had no social constructs or structure. He was innately rude and started stuff unconsciously. Khalil now felt obligated to think for the BOTH of them.

"Yeah I got Mr. G for a lawyer!"

"You got Mr. G! He's too cold with it! You are definitely gonna get up out this jam. I gotta rock it out with this PB. Hopefully she don't try to send me up the creek without a paddle."

Khalil began to think to himself.

I CANNOT let Ralph have a public defender. Their job is to help send you to jail, but I'm going to be taking on a hefty bill trying to pay his lawyer cause he ain't got it.

"I can try and see if I can get you in tune with Mr. G, but you gotta come with some bread. Mr. G don't play when it comes to that lawyer fee."

Ralph looked like a kid on Christmas.

"Man Khalil I can't thank you enough. I'm gonna make sure my girl or somebody stands on that bread to make sure he gets paid."

Khalil nodded his head in agreement, but he knew that it was going to be difficult for Ralph.

He didn't really have a support system. Hopefully they would come through long enough for the case to get dismissed or the sentencing.

"It's all good Ralph, they just have to stand on the payments, because I can't do anything from in here."

Ralph agreed and was about to continue his conversation, but was cut off by the CO's voice

"LOCK UP!!!!"

"Man Khalil this morning chow is over, but I got to holla at you when we come back out. Things ain't been playing out right out there, and I'm starting to think something fishy is going on!"

Khalil just soaked everything in that Ralph had said. He knew things were going to begin to get ugly but he didn't think it would start this early!

"It's all good Ralph! We will chop it up when they pop the locks for the day. Meet me right here!"

Khalil got up and began to take the walk back to his cell. He looked at the oatmeal colored walls filled with dirt prints and began to feel his mood start to shift. He quickly shook his head and said

"I will not let this situation get the best of me! No matter where my physical location is I am in control of me!"

Khalil continued to walk the long dirt stained hall until he reached his cell. He proceeded to enter, but hesitated because he eyed Cell Mate having yet another comfortable defecation "party" of sorts.

Khalil wanted no parts and started to walk away when CO yelled again

"LOCK UP NOW!!!"

Khalil looked at the CO and turned his head back to the cell.

He then looked back at the CO, and reluctantly walked into the cell.

Khalil knew the importance of picking his battles, and this one was not worth the fight.

He looked at Cell Mate and shook his head.

Cell Mate knew he was breaking one of the unspoken rules. He had tried to make it before it was time for everyone to be locked back up, but the way his digestive system was set up he just couldn't finish in time.

Khalil ignored the horrid smell and laid down and faced the wall as if to disappear from the cell.

Khalil closed his eyes and thought for a moment.

"I wonder what Ralph has to say? I could almost bet it has something to do with Cheese! I'm sure he is on some mess and I'm going to get to the bottom of things!"

Manor hit the Drive in his Black on Black Supercharged Durango truck.

The truck was saucy, but incognito at the same time.

The dark tint made it difficult for you to see exactly who was in the truck which was just the way Manor liked it.

He took the quick ride from downtown to Hayes attempting to clear his mind on the way.

He had a lot going on.

He was the man in his hood and it was a war going on that he was responsible for leading.

The war had been going on for months with no end in sight.

Manor didn't care about the gun play; he was a certified gangsta ready for whatever life brought, but the war sighted a drought. Which meant Manor wasn't making any money, and the hood wasn't making any money and that was a problem.

Manor took the responsibility for himself and those around him. He literally had his hood on his shoulders. Not to mention his girl was about to give birth to his son any day, and money was running low. He was an avid saver that really didn't indulge too much in mess so he was able to put his money away, but the drought had been going on for months and with no end in sight Manor knew he had to get to the money.

He was hoping that Cheese wanted to talk about getting some money, because if it was anything else Manor had no time for it.

Manor took a right turn to make his way to Hayes.

He pulled to the courts and spotted Cheeses' car.

He threw the Durango in park and hopped in Cheeses' passenger seat.

"My boy! What's to it?" Manor said.

Cheese smiled from ear to ear.

"Nothing to it but to do it!" he replied.

"Well what's up? I ain't seen you in a minute and you call with this pressing matter."

"So...Cheese started. You know I've told you before that I am a part of the Dirty Dozen."

"Yeah. Yeah Yeah. I remember" Manor said.

"But what does that have to do with me, and didn't y'all just get in trouble with them dudes that went to school with us?"

"Slow down big fella!" Cheese was beginning to puff up.

He was getting way besides himself and Manor looked as if he was about to give him a reality check.

"No. No. Let me explain." Cheese tried to soften his tone.

"They did get in trouble for robbing those 9339 boys. I was there, but they didn't snitch on me since we were cool back in school. So everyone that I was with is in jail now fighting the case. That day all of the head members of the Dirty Dozen were there so the organization is without a head. Since I am the only one let I felt as if it was my duty to step up and take things over in Khalil's absence. I have to keep the flow of the Dirty Dozen going, but also take it to a level higher than Kh---."

Cheese mid-sentence and switched he was about to reveal more than necessary.

"I just want to take the Dirty Dozen to the next level."

Manor was beginning to question a few things.

First, how was Cheese with everyone else at the robbery, but he's not in jail?

Is he a snitch?

What's his motive?

Can he be trusted?

And what was that "Taking things to a higher level than Khalil slip?"

Does he have a personal vendetta?

Is he trying to prove a point?

Manor was very adamant about minding his own business, because involving yourself in another person's mess could get you killed.

Manor took a mental note of everything Cheese alluded to and proceeded with the conversation.

"So what do you want from me?" asked Manor

. Cheese said "I need you to help me take the organization to the next level. You are the ONLY person I can trust! I am trying to make this thing worldwide so everybody knows our names! We've been getting a whole lot of money hand over fist, but we could get more!"

A thought interjected into Manor's mind.

Strike number 3!

"I don't know what Cheese is on, but he's starting to look a little fluky to me!"

"I don't care about anybody knowing my name. I actually would prefer for them NOT to know my name. I just want to get to the money! Nothing more nothing less! I got a slew of people depending on me to make something happen!"

"Cheese I don't know what your vision for this organization is, but up until this point you have been solid in my eyes. Does this opportunity allow me to get to some money though, because if not I'm not going to be able to take you up on your offer I have a full plate right now!!"

Cheese chuckled a hearty laugh as usual and replied "Does it allow you to get money?

HA. HA!!!

"Money is the motive Manor!"

"That's what this is ALL about! The cars, clothes, and chicks are just an added bonus."

Manor thought for a moment.

He felt like it was way more to the story than what Cheese was revealing.

He made it his business to keep an extra ear to the streets and his eyes focused on Cheese, but he needed the opportunity to get to the bread!

"You can count me in then Cheese! I gotta a lot of people to feed the whole hood is depending on me."

As soon as Cheese was about to open his mouth to reply his phone began to vibrate.

He dug in the pocket of his Amiri jeans and looked at the cell phone screen.

BETTY.

Cheese made a fake smirk for Manor, but he really didn't want to talk to Betty.

She was trying her best to get Khalil out of jail and Cheese wanted him to stay right where he was.

"Betty what's to it?"

Betty took a deep breath and replied "What's the game plan for the 9339 boys. We need to come up with some course of action so we can get them to not show up to court so Khalil can be free!"

Cheese acted as if he cared so deeply.

"I know Betty, I want Khalil out just as bad as you, but how are we going to approach the situation? Maybe we should just leave them out of this?"

"LEAVE THEM OUT!!!! LEAVE THEM OUT!!! Betty screamed.

"How do we leave the plaintiff's out of a case?

Manor could not believe the sabotage he was hearing.

He didn't personally know Khalil, but he knew Cheese wasn't trying at all to get Khalil out of that jam.

" I was thinking maybe it wasn't the smartest idea to try and pay them off! What if they trick about that? It will add more time or what if they just get on bullshit period we can't take chances with their lives." Cheese tried to quickly clean up his mistake.

"Well Cheese I already hinted at the idea of them being paid off and they were all for it!! They said they wanted $50,000!! $10,000 a piece for the "leaders" of the crew and they would handle the rest!!" Betty proclaimed.

"$50,000! These niggas gotta be outta of they mind! Why the hell would I pay them $50,000!"

Manor began to show a look of disgust. See he was a ride or die for his guys. SO if somebody ONLY wanted $50,000 to free his guys he was on it!!!

Cheese caught wind of Manor's disposition and tried to switch it up quickly. "Damn Betty I'm tripping, meet me at Hayes right now I got $10,000. Tell them I'll give them $10,000 a week until they are paid off." After talking Cheese looked to Manor to see if he believed what he just said.

Manor slightly believed him, but not all together.

Cheese could feel the tension. He thought to himself. "Damn I'm going to have to cough up this $10,000 in front of Manor so he knows I'm forreal!! I'll prolong this conversation until Betty gets here and he'll see me give her the money and it will look like I'm really trying to get these niggas out!"

Manor felt like Cheese was full of shit, but he was going to stick around to see if the money exchange was really going to happen.

"This nigga has been playing me all this time now he wants to call and give me some money for this case." Thought Betty.

"I've had enough of the back and forth and if it wasn't for Khalil's life being on the line I would have been said FUCK THIS!! Cheese has TOO much going on" Betty thought as she hopped on Lake Shore Drive at 39th. It would take her 15 minutes to get to Cheese, but he had played her so many times when it was time to pick up the pay off money she didn't even believe that he would be at Hayes.

"I'll give him the benefit of the doubt, but I'm sick of being in the middle...." Betty's thought was interrupted by the ringing of her cell phone.

"Hello."

"Hey Baby! What's up?"

"Hey Taron. I'm on my way to pick up the money for you right now!"

"Betty please! Those niggas are on bullshit! They don't have any money! How many times have they sent you off?"

"Six."

"Exactly SIX!! Clearly they don't want to be free or they would cough up that bread so we could let the case go. The last thing we are thinking about is them! They brought up the money and I convinced our leader to agree. You told me this would be a smooth transition. But this has been pure bullshit from the beginning. If I was to keep it ALL the way 100 with you I don't even think dude is going to accept the bread anymore."

"WHAT THE FUCK!!!! I've been playing my part! I can only handle Betty and no one else! If Cheese keeps sending me off what am I supposed to do! I consistently call and he ignores me. I'm quite sick of being in the middle anyway. I'm on my way to him to pick up $10,000 and I'll call you when I'm done!"

"Betty. Wait."

Betty hung up the phone so swiftly Laron could barely get his sentence out. She made her right turn into Hayes and looked for the Green Concorde.

She finally spotted the car, and parked next to it.

Betty looked to the right and saw Cheese smiling from ear to ear.

She looked slightly past Cheese to the passenger side and spotted Manor, a man she knew from High School. She smiled and exited the vehicle.

Betty grabbed the handle of the door on the back seat of the vehicle.

She hopped inside the peanut butter inside of the Concorde and situated herself to her comfort.

Cheese turned around and smiled.

"What's up Betty?"

Manor followed suit. He turned around and said "What's to it Betty? I haven't seen you in years!"

Betty smiled and waved at Manor. She thought Manor was a standup dude and didn't want him to bear witness to what was about to take place next.

Betty then took a deep breath and started....

"What the fuck is the problem Cheese? I've been calling you like crazy, and you've been ignoring me!! How the fuck do you expect these niggas to take care of Khalil and the crew if you aren't even doing your part? You're just NOW coming with $10,000!!!"

Cheese was pissed! "This Bitch couldn't wait until we were alone to say this shit! She's going to scare Manor off! How the fuck do I save face? He thought to himself about a quick reply.

"It's been rough on the block. I ain't been really getting money like that and I've been trying to make it happen for Khalil, Ralph, and LB. These people ain't been coming through with their end of it!!"

Manor looked to Cheese. He was perplexed at how much this nigga lied. He could recall just 20 minutes prior that Cheese had said they were getting money hand over fist.

Cheese felt Manor's peering eyes and gave him a small nod as if to tell him he was lying to Betty.

Betty continued! "Look at this point they starting not to want y'all money anymore, because they feel like it's bullshit!"

BINGO though Cheese. "If they don't want the money they are going to show up for court and Khalil is going down!!!"

Cheese put on his best acting skills "They don't want the money? They have to take it." He said in an over exaggerated tone. Cheese continued "There has already been two court cases and they are expected to be at the next!" "They can't show up!"

Betty schoffed. "Listen I've been playing my part! It's time for you to play yours!! Give me the money, and it better all be there!"

Cheese handed over the brown paper bag filled with countless bills totaling $10,000. He avoided hesitation because of Manners' presence.

"This is the last dime they will get from me. They can count on that!! Cheese thought to himself.

Manner turned and faced forward. "This dude is far from real! What the hell did I get myself into with him? He's a fake, but can I turn this situation to my favor? Or is it even worth it? He thought to himself. His thoughts were quickly interrupted.

"Bye, and answer the phone when I call it's usually important my nigga. Betty screamed as she exited the car and slammed the car door.

"What type of operation you got going here Cheese?" Manor stated matter of factly.

Cheese replied arrogantly. "A winning one!"

Chapter 22

Today was the day. Mr. G had appeared to all the required court dates and up until this time 9339 boys were not required to show. If they came to testify today the Judge would listen to their testimonies and offer up his sentence. If they didn't show the state would decide whether or not they would pick up the case or let Khalil, Ralph, and LB go.

Khalil couldn't wait to call Cadence. He knew she was still a little angry over the girlfriend situation, but it was over between him and the girl as quickly as it started.

Khalil needed to get up for breakfast and make two calls.

One to Cadence and one to Betty.

He went for his usual portion of morning slop and joined the phone line.

Khalil decided to call Betty first to get the semantics out the way. He knew it was early, but she usually answered anytime for Khalil knowing it was about business.

Today however was different!

Khalil called Betty twice before she picked up.

"Hello." Betty groggily answered.

"TOP OF THE MORNING!!! Today is a GREAT day" Khalil exclaimed through the receiver.

Khalil was avid about praying for the best and expecting the worst.

The latter was about to hit him like a ton of bricks.

"Khalil you sound so happy." Betty exclaimed, trying to have the same sense of happiness to her voice.

"So what's the move Betty?" "Your boyfriend and them coming or what?"

There was a long silence.

Khalil knew there was a problem.

"BETTY!!!" Khalil screamed.

Betty started reluctantly.

"Khalil I honestly don't know what's going to happen. Cheese was supposed to pay them $50,000 hush money. He only came with 10. I have been riding down on the block, calling, and texting him to no avail!"

Khalil looked at the receiver and thought "I'm definitely going to jail! How long is the question?"

Khalil then switched his thoughts to Cheese. "I can't believe this Nigga would be on this type of bullshit, and play with my life! It is what it is!"

Khalil's thoughts were interrupted by Betty's voice.

"Khalil!"

"Yeah!" Khalil replied.

"Thanks for everything Betty! You tried! I gotta go face the music!"

Khalil hung up the phone feeling slightly defeated.

Khalil suddenly remembered he had to call Cadence.

The phone rang once.

"Hello!"

"Cadence baby it's me Khalil!"

Cadence laughed heartily.

"Who else would it be?"

Khalil let out a small chuckle.

"Cadence Cheese didn't make good on paying the 9339 boys!"

"I'm going to jail!"

Cadence choked back her tears. She knew she had to be strong for Khalil.

"Okay baby!" Cadence uttered.

"Make sure you're at court today! It looks good for me to have family there because sentencing will take place today!"

"I haven't missed a court date yet Khalil. I'm here for you. The LONG WAY!!"

Khalil knew Cadence was being sincere. She loved him and he knew it was genuine.

"I'll see you in the courtroom Cadence. I need to go get my thoughts together. I Love you!"

Cadence wanted to continue talking, but Khalil had a lot on his mind.

Khalil hung up the phone, and contemplated calling Cheese.

He knew Cheese was a bitch and wouldn't confess to the underhanded moves, but he decided to call anyway.

Khalil picked up the phone and dialed Cheese's number.

The phone rang twice.

Cheese answered.

"Yooooooo." Cheese said sinisterly.

"This bitch ass nigga!" Khalil thought to himself.

"Cheese what's the move?" Khalil said angrily.

Cheese could hear the anger in Khalil's voice and proceeded with caution. Although Khalil was going to jail Cheese knew he would eventually have an out date, and he wasn't prepared for any smoke.

"What do you mean Khalil?"

"Hump." Khalil said with a body jerk and head nod.

"What do I mean? Why the fuck didn't you take them niggas the money to handle the business?"

Cheese became a horrible actor.

"Man K! I've been trying to get at them niggas for weeks. I've been calling, dropping by the clothing store, and texting. They been dodging me! I even been on Betty bumper and she acting like she don't want no parts of this shit! What was I supposed to do?"

Cheese hoped Khalil believed his lies!

Khalil paused for a moment.

"Man Cheese that shit is CAP!!!! This the same shit they telling me they trying to do with you, and you dodging them!"

"It's all good though!" "I just need niggas to play their part while I'm in here! I ain't in no position to hold no grudge on a Nigga from right here, but you showed your hand and I see who you are forreal!"

"Damn." Cheese thought.

"This wasn't supposed to play out like this!" "I gotta clean this up!"

"I don't know about this show your hand shit you're talking, but I do know I got you while you're in there. You're my brother for sure!" Cheese said convincingly.

Khalil laughed deeply.

"I would hate to see your enemy! But thanks! I gotta go get this time so I'll get back at you when I can!"

Cheese started to feel a bit or remorse for his actions.

Khalil had been nothing, but 100 with him.

Cheese quickly shook the thought and replied.

"Alright my dude and hung up the phone."

Khalil returned the receiver to the phone post and looked at the long line behind him.

He dared a nigga to even breathe to hard, and he was going to clear their ass right there.

Khalil proceeded to sit on the bench for the courtroom line up. This was going to be a long morning!

"KHALIL KING, RALPH PAUL, MALCOLM "LB" KING." The guard shouted from the front of the cells in the back of the courtroom.

Khalil, Ralph, and LB were uncuffed and walked towards the courtroom door.

The guard turned to Khalil as she had grown fond of his character in the past few months.

"The Judge is having a bad ass day!!" She exclaimed.

Khalil dropped his head. "Just what the fuck I needed! Mr. G told me this was a law Judge. I hope he is on business!" He thought to himself.

Khalil walked into the courtroom and looked to his left.

The courtroom was crowded with familiar and unfamiliar faces.

Khalil spotted Nadine and Cadence sitting together.

He offered a head nod and a slight smile.

He looked a tad to his left and saw Cheese.

"The nerve of this Nigga!" Khalil thought.

Khalil noticed all of his sisters and his nieces and nephews. The courtroom was full of support for him.

Once he reached the Judge he looked across the courtroom and saw ALL five 9339 members. He was fuming on the inside. He stared at them with death rays, and they couldn't even look him in the eyes. They knew they were wrong, and they shouldn't be doing this.

Khalil then focused his attention to the Judge.

"You all are here before me so I am able to hear the facts of this case. The Plaintiffs are here to tell their side of the story, and I will fully look at all of the details of the case. I will then proceed to my chambers to go over the letter of the law and then give you a judgement. Do you three understand?"

Khalil, Ralph, and LB simultaneously said "Yes!"

The Judge then turned to the Plaintiffs.

You may take the stand to tell your side of the story.

The leader stood and began to walk quickly to the stand first.

He sat down and the Judge proceeded.

"Do you promise to tell the truth, the whole truth so help you God?"

The leader nodded his head and said "Yes."

The Judge proceeded.

"Tell me what happened."

Khalil listened intently.

The leader began talking.

Khalil thought in his head "LIE."

"That did happen!"

"LIE."

"LIE."

Khalil couldn't believe all the lies he was hearing. They were really trying to put them away.

The leader then began to point his fingers to point out Khalil, Ralph, and LB.

The Judge interjected.

"I don't need to hear anymore."

"Do the Defendants have anything to say on their behalf?"

Mr. G approached the stand.

He turned around and started.

"Judge this was a simple fight taken entirely too far. My client Khalil King is an asset to society! He is in Barber School, active in his community, and lives with his mother Nadine."

Nadine stood and slowly approached the swinging doors of the courtroom separating the guards, defendants, plaintiffs, and Judge from the people.

Nadine looked softly and held back her tears.

Mr. G continued.

"My client got caught up at the wrong place at the wrong time. He never yielded a weapon, and although he has a background from when he was a juvenile he has been on the straight and narrow in adulthood."

"I ask for the courts mercy in sentencing today, as all of these people will be affected by Khalil King's absence in their life."

At this time everyone that came for Khalil proudly stood to be accounted for on his behalf. The courtroom was basically standing in attendance.

Cheese sat!

Khalil turned around and saw all the faces there to represent him, and he began to be saddened.

"I have a lot of people depending on me." Khalil thought.

"Look at Cheeses' bitch ass sitting down! Damn this is what it comes to!"

Mr. G wrapped up.

"Please if you can find it in your heart Judge. Take mercy!"

Ralph and LB were appointed the same public defenders, because they could not afford representation.

The PB began.

"My clients both graduated highschool, live with their mothers, and don't have kids." "This will be their first round of offenses and we ask for the least possible time. Thank You!"

"Damn this Bitch might as well hand them the book herself." Khalil thought.

"I wish I would have had the money to pay for their lawyer, but I can't save everybody!!" Khalil continued with his thoughts he was interrupted by the Judges words.

"We will take a small intercession. I will go to my chambers and review the facts of the case. I will look at the letter of the law and we will reconvene in 30 minutes."

Khalil looked back at Cadence,

Cadence faked a smile.

Khalil faked one in return.

Khalil, Ralph, and LB were taken back into the holding cells of the court. Everyone else in the courtroom sat and waited.

Thirty Minutes took a lifetime. Cadence and Nadine took a washroom break.

Nadine looked to Cadence and spoke.

"Khalil will be fine! It will all work out Jehovah has him."

Cadence wanted to believe her so badly. She wanted Khalil home and in her arms, but she knew that it was far fetched. All she could hope for was the least possible time.

Cadence and Nadine returned to the courtroom just in time to hear the Bailiff.

"Please stand for the honorable Judge Wavy."

Judge Wavy walked in looking very serious.

Cadence got very scared.

The Judge spoke.

"I would like to recall the case with Khalil King, Ralph Paul, and Malcolm "LB" King."

The guard screamed their names to the top of his lungs and slowly Khalil, Ralph, and LB appeared.

The Judge began.

"Malcolm. You used excessive force in this manner. You brought a gun to a hand fight, and I am perplexed as to why. You have a background and don't have much going on for yourself. I want you to use this time I'm giving you wisely to better yourself, and come out to be an asset to society."

"You are sentenced to 12 years in the Cook County Department of Corrections. Please be wise with your time."

The courtroom gasped.

12 years! That was A LOT of time.

The Judge continued interrupting everyone's thoughts.

"Ralph to the stand please. As I review the facts of the case, and look at the video footage you seem to be very involved and very aggressive. I almost get the notion that you liked some of the activities that took place. After looking into your background I see that this is not uncommon territory for you. I would also recommend that you use your time wisely. Enter a drug program, get a GED, or pick up a trade."

"You are sentenced to 10 years in the Cook County Department of Corrections. Again use this time wisely to better yourself and come out and be an asset to society."

The courtroom was in complete despair.

Cadence was already crying. "The years that this Judge is giving out is insane! I'm at a loss for words!" Cadence thought to herself. " I just..."

Cadence's thoughts were interrupted by the Judge.

"Khalil.

The Judge looked at Khalil with a look of disgust.

He began to speak "After reviewing the details of this case and all of the preponderance of evidence placed before me I have no choice but to invoke a strict sentence. Khalil dropped his head in disappointment. His biggest fear was playing out right before his eyes and he knew in his gut that things were not going to play out in his favor. He listened as the Judge continued.

"You have been given chance, after chance, after chance."

"As a juvenile you have committed crimes that the courts have forgiven you of. I believe that it is high time that you and the rest of the parties associated with this case learn a very valuable lesson about being a positive asset to our society."

"I do understand that you in this particular instance were NOT the individual holding the gun, and I also understand that no one got harmed in this ridiculous display of masculinity."

"HOWEVER, the record that proceeds you is one of small acts of violence and gun play. It seems to me that you are progressively getting more confident in your criminal ways and it is my duty to give you a reality check."

"With all that being said I am sentencing you to 8 YEARS in the Cook County Department of Corrections."

"Again I hope that you use this time wisely and become an asset to society. Enter a drug program, get a GD, or practice barbering. I would also recommend getting a new set of friends, because they got you in this mess!"

Khalil began to tear up out of anger!

"All of this for nothing!"

"8 years! 8 years!"

"How would he survive 8 years behind bars?"

"Who would stick by his side for 8 ENTIRE years?"

"How could his life ever be the same?"

All Khalil knew at this point was that he had A LOT of time ahead of him to figure it out!

Thank You for reading

Addicted To Love:
An Eastside Love Story

Be on the lookout for
TOO ADDICTED TO LOVE in Fall 2020.